THE NIGHTMARE MURDERS

Following a strange compulsion, Robert Harcourt finds himself consulting a fortune teller who gives him a sinister message. He says he sees Robert in a mansion, surrounded by happy faces. There is a woman, a beautiful woman. Robert is attracted to her, but hurts her cruelly, and so deeply that she will never forgive him. That very night, as the clock strikes the hour of midnight, Robert will take the life of a man dear to her. He will become — *a murderer*!

GERALD VERNER

◆

THE NIGHTMARE MURDERS

Complete and Unabridged

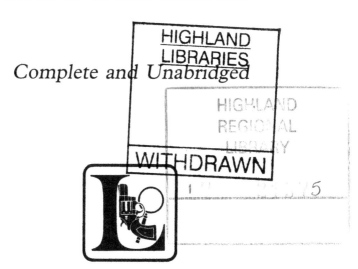

LINFORD
Leicester

First published in Great Britain

First Linford Edition
published 2018

A catalogue record for this book is available
from the British Library.

ISBN 978–1–4448–3669–1

Published by
F. A. Thorpe (Publishing)
Anstey, Leicestershire

Set by Words & Graphics Ltd.
Anstey, Leicestershire
Printed and bound in Great Britain by
T. J. International Ltd., Padstow, Cornwall

This book is printed on acid-free paper

1

The Black Room

Big Ben boomed the hour of four as darkness gradually descended upon London. Lights flickered here and there; electric signs in Leicester Square flashed to life; street lamps came on; shop windows were lit; headlights glared; theatres and cinemas, surrounded by their glittering brilliance, shone through the gloom; and the long December evening had begun.

In one of the still-dark streets behind Shaftesbury Avenue, Robert Harcourt, having partaken of the last of many drinks, was laboriously endeavouring to find his way to these bright lights. He was badly drunk — and he knew it. He'd set out that morning with the express purpose of getting drunk and he'd succeeded, albeit his pocket was a bit lighter and his head a bit heavier. He caught hold of a lamp-post nearby to steady himself, and stood leaning against it, breathing heavily and feeling sick.

'Damned fool,' he growled under his breath. His head was splitting. Everything was swimming before his eyes. 'Why did I do it?' he asked himself.

Thelma! The name cut through his consciousness like a rush of cold water. Of course — Thelma! He was spending every penny he had to try and forget her, to stop thinking about her. But he couldn't get away from her even when he was drunk. Strangely enough, this thought seemed to revive him, and the blackness before his eyes ceased to dance. No, it was no use trying to escape, he decided; one just had to put up with it.

He suddenly pulled himself together and began walking more or less steadily down the street. He *did* have something else to occupy his mind. The fortune teller! He must go, now, this very minute, before leaving town . . .

At last! Lights, people, traffic. He looked up and blinked. He was opposite the taxi rank in Shaftesbury Avenue. He fumbled in his pocket for the address

— at last he found it. Still feeling far from sober, he walked up to the nearest taxi and pushed the piece of paper before the driver's eyes. 'Take me there, will you?' he said thickly.

The driver gave a gruff laugh. 'Going to a fortune teller, sir? Sure you feel well enough?'

'Take me there, do you hear?' Robert repeated, angrily. 'Nine, Queen's Court, Bloomsbury.'

'Right, sir. You know best.'

Robert pushed the piece of paper back into his pocket and staggered towards the door.

'Careful, sir,' cautioned the driver with a grin as he opened it for him.

Robert staggered onto the seat inside, and the driver slammed the door behind him. The taxi swept along in the direction of Bloomsbury.

What a day! Robert reflected as he sank back against the cushions. An entire day spent among acquaintances and so-called friends; in pubs and those numerous little clubs that seemed to have sprung up all over London, like some infectious disease.

And all the time, two thoughts were uppermost in his mind. He might be laughing, listening to a questionable tale told by one of his companions; growing sentimental over a barmaid; but always there at the back of his mind were those two thoughts, those two people — Thelma and Omar.

Thelma was the woman he had loved, but who had told him to pull himself together, to throw up the set and the endless round of futility to which his wealth had led him. She, who had thrown his ring back in his face and told him that he was the greatest disappointment of her life. She had deserted him, and at the moment when his wealth had deserted him also.

For only two days later he had been informed by his lawyers that his period of extravagance had come to an end; that from now on he must live moderately and all his 'luxuries' must be paid for by the sweat of his brow. They told him that all he could rely upon from his late father's estate was sufficient to keep a roof over his head, while anything outside that he must find for himself. If he wanted to enjoy himself, he must work. But what at? That was the question.

He was idle and useless. Something must be done. But what? He couldn't think.

Then he hit on the idea — he would drown his sorrows! Destitute of his sweetheart and his fortune, the only thing left to do was to get drunk. The masculine method of dodging the issue.

It was then that the idea that had been vaguely at the back of his mind for the past three days had unexpectedly risen to the surface. *Omar!*

Omar was a fashionable fortune teller: that much he knew. He had his address in his pocket. But how he had first heard of the name and when or why he had written down the address, he couldn't remember.

'You're here, sir.' The voice of the taxi driver broke in upon his meditations.

Robert fell out of the taxi in confusion. 'Fell out' is the only adequate description of his hurried and completely undignified exodus. In front of him was a tall, rambling old house, over the door of which was painted in bright new lettering the name 'Omar'. And underneath, in

5

smaller letters — 'Palmist and fortune teller'.

He turned to the taxi driver. 'How much?'

The man, putting his hand over the meter, said something quite monstrous, but Robert didn't bat an eyelid as he handed the man a note. 'Keep the change.'

The man grinned. 'Thank you, sir. Good night.'

The taxi slid out of sight. Robert turned towards the building again. Five floors. He counted them automatically. 'Wonder what he does with the other four,' he thought, noticing the uncurtained windows and dirty frames.

He walked up to the door and stabbed the bell. While waiting for a reply, he again relapsed into his former reverie. Tall, flat roofed houses on every side of him — offices most likely; and here, in an apparently empty house, was Omar, the well-known society fortune teller. Yet in spite of all this, he wasn't surprised. It all seemed to follow on in some mysterious way, as though it had been planned beforehand.

'What can I do for you, sir?'

Robert came back to earth abruptly. In front of him stood a little man, faultlessly dressed in a dark lounge suit, who was the possessor of the extremely ingratiating voice.

'I — er — I want to see Mr. Omar, please.'

'Have you an appointment, sir?'

'No, I'm afraid not. But I've been recommended by somebody — '

'By whom, sir?'

'I — I can't remember.' Robert looked at him hopelessly.

'I see, sir.' The man turned to go.

'No, don't go,' Robert cried desperately. 'Here, give him this.' He thrust his card into the man's hand. 'It'll be all right when he sees that,' he went on breathlessly. 'He's expecting me.'

'Very well, sir. If you'll wait a few moments, I'll see what can be done.' With the same air of faultless politeness, he pushed the door to and retreated into the darkness of the passage beyond.

Robert pulled out his handkerchief and mopped his brow. He looked at his wristwatch. Quarter to five. He had to be down at the Fredericks' place in the country in about three hours, so this Omar chap had better get a move on.

The obsequious little man returned. 'Will you step this way, sir?'

Evidently the card had worked! Robert crossed the threshold and the little man closed the front door.

'This way, sir.' He passed in front of him and led the way through the darkness.

Robert's feet sank into the most luxurious carpet at every step. But not a sign of illumination did he see all the way.

At length the little man opened a door, ushering him into a large room apparently decorated in black from floor to ceiling. The only illumination was a heavily shaded central light, below which, in the brilliant circle, stood a solitary armchair.

'Will you sit down, sir?'

Robert moved towards the armchair. With a slight bow, the little man walked back towards the door by which they had entered. 'You will not be kept waiting long, sir,' he said. He slipped noiselessly from sight, closing the door behind him.

Robert looked round the large room. Walls, door, ceiling — all were the deepest black. There were only two chairs, the other an upright one by a table just outside the radius of the circle cast by the light. There was no other furniture and apparently no window. With a sigh of resignation, he walked across to the armchair and sat down.

He'd begun to feel quite pleasantly sleepy. The moment he sat in the armchair, he had the odd feeling that he was doing everything under orders. He looked towards the other chair — the upright, high backed one at the opposite end of the table — and wondered sleepily why he had not seated himself in that one, instead of settling himself where he was. He was on the verge of falling off altogether when he was disturbed by a deep, sonorous voice.

'You are Mr. Robert Harcourt? You were sent to me?'

'Yes.'

'But you cannot remember by whom?'

'No.'

The voice was coming from the far end of the room; this much he could detect. Perhaps this one he was in now was merely a part of a much larger room, partitioned off. And Omar was behind that partition speaking to him through a microphone . . .

Robert was feeling extraordinarily impressed. He had suddenly become conscious that he was under observation. Sitting as he was, every movement, every expression must be clearly visible to anyone outside the radius of the light. In fact, it was just like being in a showcase.

'You wish me to foretell the future?'

'Yes.'

The feeling of acting under orders seemed to be intensifying. He was offering no resistance now, and his drowsiness deepened.

'Very well. In a few seconds I will be with you.'

Robert waited. All was silent. Now no curiosity stirred within him, and he failed to notice a cunningly concealed door at the opposite end of the room, slowly opening, until it was wide enough to admit the owner of the voice that had so recently lulled him into drowsy security with its silken tones. The door slid noiselessly back into position as the figure of a man advanced slowly into the room. He was tall, dressed in some long, flowing robe, and over his face he wore a mask through which his eyes — feverishly bright, like living coals — gleamed with a strange fanaticism. He moved towards the table. In his outstretched hands he held a crystal. He seated himself in the high-backed chair, placing the crystal upon the table before him.

Robert sat with his head thrown back, his eyes half-shut, staring up towards the shadowy blackness of the ceiling. Then Omar spoke.

'Look into my eyes.' The words constituted an order, but the tones were still as silken as ever.

Robert obeyed. His eyes moved down from the ceiling until they focused themselves upon those of the man facing him.

'You came here tonight because you

had no choice,' the voice continued. 'You were ordered to come. Is that so?'

'That is so.'

Robert's eyes, now wide, were staring, quite expressionless. Omar raised the crystal in his hands. 'Look with me into this crystal.'

The crystal gleamed as though with hidden fires.

'Now I will tell you what I see.' Two sets of eyes were fixed upon the glowing object. 'I see you in a beautiful mansion surrounded by happy faces, by festivities and joyfulness,' Omar intoned seductively. 'Laughter is in the air. There is a woman there — a beautiful woman. Do you know her?'

'Yes.'

There was a note of pain in that one word. For a fleeting moment, Robert's voice became alive before returning to its former flatness.

'You are attracted to her, but you hurt her. Cruelly, you hurt her. This very night I can see you hurting her so deeply that she will never forgive you. This very night.'

'This very night,' Robert repeated.

'I will tell you how you will hurt her.' The voice of the fortune teller grew hard and ominous. 'This night, as the clock strikes the hour of midnight, you will take the life of a man dear to her. You will become a — murderer!'

The last word was uttered in a harsh, accusing whisper. Robert repeated it, dully. 'A murderer!'

Omar leant forward. 'Do you understand that?'

'I understand it,' came the reply.

Something like a sigh of satisfaction broke from the fortune teller. And his voice, from this point onwards, assumed an even stronger note of command. 'You will decide to kill this man on the instant. You will wait until midnight; then you will creep to his bedroom. He will be asleep. You will go to his bed . . . '

'Go to his bed.' Robert's voice chimed in like a child repeating a lesson.

' . . . and you will strangle him. With your bare hands!' There was a pause. Drops of sweat stood out upon the fortune teller's brow. Yet when he spoke, his voice was as steady as before. 'Repeat that.'

'I shall strangle him — with my bare hands.' There was something infinitely pathetic about the ghastly, passionless way in which these words were spoken.

Placing the crystal back upon the table, the fortune teller once more fixed Robert with his burning gaze. 'And now, I shall give you a sign by which you will know your victim. Listen to me carefully.' He drew a deep breath before proceeding in the same terrible monotone. 'The man whom you are about to kill will wear a diamond ring upon the second finger of his left hand.'

'A diamond ring,' Robert repeated drowsily.

'The man you will kill!'

'That man I shall kill!'

Omar rose from his seat. His whole attitude was one of excessive relief. He moved over to Robert, smiling faintly. 'And now forget that you have ever been here!'

Slowly he raised his arms as though to make some passes.

* ★ *

. . . Strangle with bare hands — kill — murderer — midnight — diamond ring! Dreadful thoughts rushing through his brain. Unheard-of ideas planted in his consciousness. A man towering above him, a crystal, hands moving in front of his eyes. From blackness to light — from light to blackness, then — a laugh. A devilish, triumphant laugh brought him hurtling through the fiendish mirages of unreality back to the macabre, awe-inspiring spectacle of the black room.

Robert opened his eyes. He was in the armchair. The light was still above his head; the shadows still enveloped everything around him. He sat up, blinked, and looked again. He was alone.

An awful pain shot through his head. If only he could think! What had happened to him? Where had he been?

The pain in his head increased to such an alarming extent that further thought became impossible. Fortunately, this being the zenith of his torture, it passed as quickly as it had come; and although it

15

left him limp and exhausted, his brain began to function again.

At first he felt inclined to look upon the whole thing as a nightmare. Indeed, he almost persuaded himself that the fortune teller hadn't been to him at all. But then he remembered. A voice through a microphone! It was all coming back! The voice (which he took to be Omar's) had asked his name, and what he wanted, and then — then he had said he was coming in. But what had happened afterwards?

Slowly he began to remember certain sentences; somebody prophesying something. Then Omar *had* been in to him! He thought again, and this time the words took on a new significance. They appeared not only as a prophecy, but as a command. Something he had been commanded to do. That he must do, something as inevitable as fate. But what was it?

He buried his head in his hands. What was it? He was striving to remember with every nerve in his mind.

Suddenly he jumped to his feet, a quickly suppressed cry of horror springing to his lips. He knew! The words he had found difficulty in remembering only a few seconds ago were now emblazoned before his terror-stricken eyes in letters of fire.

'It can't be true,' he kept telling himself. 'I fell asleep. I dreamed it. I can't believe it!'

He began savagely pacing the room. Frantically he endeavoured to reason with himself. Then his attention was caught by something bright on the table. It was the crystal!

It only took this to convince him of what he already knew to be true; there was no further argument. When he first entered that room, the table had been bare. Now this crystal was standing upon it. Somebody had brought it in. And who would have done that, but Omar?

He stood looking at it for some seconds without moving. Then he put his hand into his pocket. The slip upon which he'd written the address was missing. So it was true!

Unobtrusively, the door behind him slowly opened; the little man who had admitted him stepped into the room.

'Have you finished, sir?' he enquired smoothly. Robert turned to him and felt inclined to laugh; it seemed so incongruous that in the midst of his nightmare, he should persist in meeting this absurd little man.

'Yes. I've finished,' he managed to say.

With a polite smile, the man stood aside for him to pass.

Robert walked slowly towards the door. On reaching it, he suddenly burst into a roar of laughter. For he'd just thought of his drunkenness and how he couldn't remember who'd sent him. 'Of course, that's it,' he cried, turning to the little man. 'I'm drunk. Drunk!' He burst into a roar of laughter, but the man remained unmoved.

Suddenly he stopped and looked round the room again. As he did so, that odd haunted look returned to his eyes. He drew in his breath; and without saying another word, turned on his heel and ran madly down the passage.

The slam of the front door indicated that Robert had left the house.

2

Virginia

The fresh air eventually revived him, but when he came to his senses again he was in unfamiliar surroundings. After making several inquiries, he managed to find his way to a taxi rank, where he was surprised to find that he was in the neighbourhood of Islington.

Virginia Fredericks had been on the point of ringing the bell of Number Nine, Queen's Court at the precise moment when Robert rushed headlong out of the passage into the ill-lit street beyond. The fact of seeing him there was surprising, as was the state he was in. She slipped past him into the passage, just missing the door as he slammed it to.

Alone in the darkness, she gave a nervous little laugh. She could hardly believe it. Robert, at a fortune teller's! And his face! Such a terrified expression

19

as she'd never seen there before!

'Won't Thelma be surprised,' she thought. Then she stopped. Perhaps that was the cause of it. She knew her step-sister had just broken off her engagement with Robert and that he'd taken it badly. She was sure he loved Thelma, and she him. What a mess! Ah well, she had enough worries of her own without taking on other people's.

Dismissing Robert from her thoughts, she tiptoed down the passage, scarcely daring to breathe. She was an intruder, and the general atmosphere of the place was sinister.

She felt as though she'd walked miles before she was halfway to her destination, and the complete lack of visibility grated on her nerves. Her only consolation was to remember with pleasure how she'd managed to slip past Robert during that fleeting moment when he had stood by the open door. Also, she had escaped the vigilance of the little man — Saunders, as she knew he was called. For days now she had been pestering him for a further interview with Omar, and every time, he had produced some new excuse to frustrate her. Either he was too busy, or too tired to see anyone. If you wrote, Saunders replied to your letter. If you phoned, Saunders answered the phone.

She remembered with regret that her first and only interview with Omar had been arranged through Saunders without difficulty. Since then, however, it had been impossible. Omar had obviously decided to make things just as difficult as he could.

Their solitary interview, she now realised, had been strange and unsatisfactory. It had lasted scarcely more than ten minutes and the great Omar did nothing more for her than she would have expected from any travelling-fair fortune teller. And this was the man whom the county flocked after! He must be making a fortune out of them. His method of having no fixed fee, but of accepting whatever they cared to give him, was inspired; the donations he received far surpassing any fee he might have named.

Omar was clever. And yet he had as good as refused her a second interview.

She'd been generous on her first visit, despite her disappointment, and surely her money was as good as anyone else's. Or was it possible that he'd guessed that she had a strong ulterior motive for wishing to see him? A motive she was so eager to gratify that she would stop at nothing — even creeping into his house unbidden, as she was doing now — to further its chances of success? Could this be the cause of his refusal?

If he had told her of some calamity about to befall her, she could have understood his distaste. However, what little he had told her had been entirely favourable, though a great deal of it she had missed, owing to the fact that he persisted in sitting in the darkness and mumbling in some kind of assumed voice she had found difficult to follow.

She suddenly found herself up against something that felt like a door. Cautiously, she put her hand forward and groped for the handle. As she caught hold of it, another doubt assailed her.

It was bad enough to force oneself into a man's house without his knowledge, but an even worse offence to force one's way into his private study, the place from which he conducted his business. She found it difficult to make up her mind. In her perplexity, she gripped the handle tightly until she suddenly made up her mind. Boldly throwing open the door, she strode into the room beyond. As she paused and looked around her, the words of greeting died upon her lips. For it was empty.

The door through which she had entered had, without her being aware of it, closed behind her, and the walls now presented an unbroken front of uniform black. So perfect was their colouring that not by the slightest hint could she guess where the door had been; the other one, into Omar's private sanctum, being likewise invisible. The whole room was producing an uncanny effect upon her. She felt lost.

Pull yourself together, she told herself. *How can you help her by behaving like this?*

In a few seconds, she was nearly her old confident self again. It was just as well; for almost on the instant, the door leading to the inner sanctum began to slide open. *So it's the watchdog again!* She smiled.

At first Saunders failed to notice her presence; she was standing in the shadows and naturally made not the slightest effort to make herself heard. He had closed the door and was practically halfway across the room before he perceived her figure near at hand. He stopped. 'Who's there?' His voice had a peremptory ring about it; an impression, increased no doubt by an ominous bulge in one of his pockets, into which he had swiftly slipped his hand.

'It's all right! Only me!' Virginia retorted cheekily as she stepped into the circle of light.

The hand was quickly withdrawn from the pocket, and instantly the mask of servility was reassumed. 'May I inquire how you managed to get in?'

'You may, watchdog,' Virginia retorted with a laugh. 'I walked in through the front door. I happened to see my dear friend, Mr. Harcourt, making his rather undignified exit — '

'Is he a friend of yours?'

'More an acquaintance, if it's all the same to you. But as I was saying; just as I was contemplating ringing the bell, I saw Mr. Harcourt fairly hurtling out of this house as though pursued by a ghost. He jumped out and I jumped in! Eureka!'

'I see.'

'I felt my way down the passage, threw open the door, and — here I am!'

'And your reason for all this?' Saunders still managed to keep his tones as respectful as ever. 'Could it be that you wish to see Mr. Omar?'

'It could! Well? Surely I'm not to be turned down again?'

'Please don't put it like that, Miss Fredericks. It's so difficult.'

Virginia took him firmly by the shoulders. 'Look here, Saunders. I've been trying to see Mr. Omar for the past fortnight. I've phoned, written and called at least half a dozen times. And you've always made it your business to prevent me. Why? Didn't I pay him enough the only time when he did see me?'

'Oh yes, I think so . . . but I don't know why he won't see you, miss. Those are his orders, and I just have to obey them. It's no affair of mine.'

'You're sure they *are* his orders?'

'Oh yes. Quite sure. He told me most definitely that he'd never give you another sitting — ever.'

'Didn't he give you any reason for this — decision, on his part?'

'No, Miss — er — Fredericks, he didn't. Perhaps it's that he foresees something fatal and doesn't want to tell you about it.'

'Surely he's got a reason stronger than that?'

'Well, I don't know it, then, miss.'

She turned away from him disconsolately, and he crossed behind her in the direction of the door. 'And now, miss, would you mind — '

'Wait a minute!' she cut him short. 'You said he wouldn't give me another sitting. That means that he refuses to foretell things for me, doesn't it? He won't read my palm, or anything?'

'That is correct, miss.'

She came over to him, her face radiant with the new idea that had just occurred to her. 'But he wouldn't refuse if you said I wanted to see him about something quite different, would he? Mr. Omar owns this entire building, doesn't he?'

'Why, yes, miss. But I don't see — '

'I want to rent one of these rooms as an office. Any objection?'

'Why no, miss. But I'm afraid Mr. Omar would never consent to such a thing.'

'Wouldn't he? Are you sure? It must cost a lot to keep all those floors empty, so what's his reason for keeping all those rooms untenanted?'

'I don't know, miss. But I do know that he'd never even consider such a tiring.'

'Anyway, there's no harm in my seeing him, is there?'

'But — excuse my asking, miss, but what would you be wanting an office for?'

'I'm a freelance journalist, my dear little man, and I want somewhere to write. My home's miles out in the country, and I loathe clubs. That O.K.? Now run along and tell Mr. Omar I'm here.'

'I'm not at all sure that I ought to, miss,' the little man put in waveringly.

But just when she felt the day was hers,

she was unexpectedly foiled. The front doorbell began to ring.

Saunders stopped immediately, glad of an excuse to get out of his uncomfortable predicament. 'Excuse me, miss.' Finding the door leading into the hall as though by instinct, he hurriedly disappeared through it.

Virginia gazed after him with an irritated sigh of despair. She was boiling with indignation. To get so far and then to fail seemed monstrous. Her victory over Saunders alone should have assured her success. Whereas at their previous meetings he had been so unapproachable, this time it had been quite simple. Of course she realised that the shock of her sudden appearance must have had a great deal to do with it; and added to that, the dictatorial manner she could always assume at will.

At times, when she was being herself, she would be feminine and charming; other times, as at present, she would be hard and masculine. Which was the real Virginia? This was the question that puzzled her father, sister and her friends.

For none of them knew the answer; and she remained an enigma to them all.

To look at, she was classically beautiful. Her hair was jet-black, thick and glistening with a glorious sheen to it. Her eyes were large, dark, and they glittered provocatively. Add to this a smooth olive complexion, a pair of naturally scarlet lips, and a slow, alluring smile that displayed gleaming white teeth.

Although her father, Benjamin Fredericks, had settled in England many years back, most of her early childhood had been spent in New York. Unfortunately for her, her father and mother were anything but happy together. So when she died, Benjamin Fredericks, being still a comparatively young man, left New York, putting his child into the hands of some wealthy relations out there, and made his way to England, hoping to leave his troubles far behind him and make a fresh start in a new land.

Not only did he make a fresh start, but he fell desperately in love for the first time in his life. The woman he loved was a widow and the mother of a little girl.

They were soon married; and little by little, his interest in Virginia evaporated. Except for an occasional line to her now and then, he forgot that she existed.

He was rudely awakened, however, when one day a beautiful young lady of seventeen arrived at his house and asked for admittance. She was his daughter, she said, and had been sent home to her father.

The relations she had stayed with for so many years had struck bad times. They wrote to Benjamin several letters imploring him to send them money to help towards the upkeep of his daughter. Deliberately or otherwise, he ignored their requests; and things soon came to such a pass that they were forced to send her, much as they disliked doing so, back to him. And so from that time forth she became his entire responsibility.

All that can be said of him is that he did everything for her that was in his power; although, quite naturally, he favoured his step-daughter — Thelma, as she was called — for she represented to him a far happier period in his life.

But unfortunately for him, this period was all too short. Less than two years after Virginia's arrival, his second wife, always inclined to be delicate, died of pneumonia after a brief struggle. And with her died a part of Benjamin's soul. He carried on as usual, and casual acquaintances might have noticed no change in him. But those who knew him well began to miss his hearty laugh and jolly manners. In their place were long periods of gloom, followed by an inexplicable sense of exhaustion. When he went to his bed at night, no desire to see the dawn found its way into his heart. The part of him that had died with his wife had left him incomplete, a shadow of a man waiting for the end.

There was only one thing that kept him alive — his love for Thelma. He had always been fond of her, but now he positively idealised her. She was all that was left to him of the woman he loved. So once again, even though they were now living under the same roof, Virginia felt herself slipping away into the background.

And so it went on from year to year. But as she grew older, she no longer missed the love and attention that should by rights have been hers. Instead, she grew up self-reliant, ambitious, and completely unspoilt, with, above all, her faith in humanity unimpaired. But in spite of this absence of ill-feeling on her part, she and her step-sister never became very good friends. They didn't dislike each other, but simply had absolutely nothing in common. They knew nothing about each other and never attempted to discover anything. Virginia went her way and the others went theirs. They were perfectly polite, and moderately happy.

By this time she was twenty-four, and had begun to write. Her father took little interest in her work. Then, to everybody's surprise, she became engaged to a man who was her opposite in every possible way. Where she was volatile and bright, he was slow and stupid. Where she was self-possessed and at her ease, he was clumsy and embarrassed. As everybody at the time declared, they certainly made a most curious couple. At first this roused everybody's interest, but after a few weeks even that died down, and once again she was left to herself, unhampered by questions or restrictions.

Her father had given to her a key to the house and her own car. Where she went, how she spent her time, or with whom she spent it, were all matters of supreme indifference to the family. Hence it was, that this woman, without anyone's knowledge or acquiescence, came to be a visitor at the house of Omar.

She began pacing the room nervously; then she looked at her watch: half past five. She'd been here half an hour already. She remembered hearing a clock somewhere strike five as she went to knock at the door.

What a long time Saunders was at the door! And who could it be, at this time? She knew Omar's interviewing hours ended at five. Saunders had informed her of that upon several occasions.

All at once she stopped her perambulation about the room; a daring smile hovered at the corners of her lips. What if she dared? Omar was only in the next room. Why not go and knock on the door? He'd probably think it was Saunders. And then she'd get a chance to . . .

But how could she find the door? She would have to feel her way round the walls. And then it was just her luck that Saunders would come back and ask her what she was doing.

'Everything clear, Saunders?'

She swung round. What on earth?

'Everything clear?'

Her moment of surprise had passed. Of course — the 'microphone'. So he was asking if the coast was clear, was he? That might mean anything.

There was a door, and it was slowly opening. The door to the inner sanctum! She began to creep round the table, preparing to meet the man she so longed to see — face to face.

She had reached the end of the table when something dull caught her eye. It was the crystal, which was still on the table. Almost unwillingly, she found herself gazing into it. Slowly, inch by inch, the door continued to open.

Without moving from where she stood, she could see a perfect reflection of the door, the room beyond — in a minute she'd be able to see the man! Yes — here he was . . .

Suddenly she gave the most piercing scream; her face, drained on the instant of every drop of blood, looked white and horrified.

There was a shot! A crash as the crystal splintered into a thousand fragments. Saunders was standing at the opposite end of the room, a smoking revolver in his hand.

But none of this did she notice, for her eyes were pinned on the door, now fully opened, and on the dark figure that was slowly advancing across the threshold to meet her!

3

The Manor House

Benjamin Fredericks' mansion was situated about thirty miles from London, five miles from the nearest railway station. It stood on a slope, screened by trees on all sides.

The site was chosen by his second wife, Helen. She worshipped the country, and her love of solitude was so strong it almost amounted to a vice. Being the only vice she had, poor soul, nobody could blame her for it. Her thirst for solitude had prompted her to seek out this desolate though beautiful spot. Built according to her design, the house was a fine building. It came as the greatest disappointment in Benjamin's life that she never lived to see it completed. Following her death, he allowed several weeks to elapse before bringing himself to carry on with the building, at Thelma's request. She had told him that it would have pleased her mother for him to continue with it, as though she were still there.

And so, six months later, the large and handsome house was completed, following his dead wife's wishes down to the minutest detail. Benjamin became the owner of a mansion of which he was justly proud, and eagerly he invited all and sundry down to see it. Tears of gratitude instantly filled his eyes when anybody praised it; and the humble assurance that it was 'all Helen's doing — God bless her — all Helen's doing', was ever on his lips.

It stood at the head of a large horseshoe drive; and with its three storeys of massive masonry, its heavily studded doors, and latticed windows, appeared a typical home of old Tudor England. Inside it was the same: large fireplaces piled with logs — candles (electric, unfortunately) in sconces fixed to the walls — oaken beams stretching across the ceilings, while in the centre of the hall stood the majestic staircase. The furniture was heavy and ornately carved; the few pictures were genuine oil paintings of the period; and the whole building exuded a definite atmosphere of its own.

Now it was ablaze with light and alive with the hum of cheerful activity. On this bleak winter's night it presented the pleasantest picture imaginable. Every window's little panes fairly glistened through the darkness. Servants were hurrying to and fro, giving finishing touches to the bedrooms, laying the large table in the dining-room; in the kitchen the cook bustled about tending the making of the most delectable dishes; the butler waited to obey the summons of the doorbell, curious as to the arrival of each newcomer. The whole place seethed with a feeling of expectation . . . and all in honour of Benjamin Fredericks' sixtieth birthday.

On this special occasion, although many acquaintances had kindly remembered him, it was only a select few who had the honour of being present to celebrate it. The guests were anything but commonplace, presenting some of the most arresting personalities, pleasant and otherwise. These favoured individuals were being admirably entertained, in the absence of their host, by his charming step-daughter, Thelma. Gathered around a blazing fire, some were sipping cocktails, others smoking. Their subject under discussion was a suicide that had occupied the front pages of the newspapers some three weeks ago but had since then faded into the limbo of forgotten cases.

It was Thelma who had started this discussion on suicide, rather in an effort to find something to say, than from any morbid interest in such cases. A beautiful, fresh-looking woman of twenty-two, she was the living image of her mother. Her naturally blonde hair, wide blue eyes, and soft, well-shaped mouth were all a constant reminder to her step-father of the woman who had gone. Even her manner, her way of talking — all were Helen. Her discretion, her good taste — which indirectly led to Benjamin calling his house 'the manor house' instead of something much more flamboyant — seemed hereditary too, yet somehow made even more charming by the addition of a lovable and unspoilt quality all her own.

She filled her place as the only woman in the party, Virginia having failed to return so far. Her easy grace entirely bewitched even the most critical of her beholders.

Sitting on the arm of her chair was Paul Conway, a vaguely unpleasant-looking young man of about thirty-five. The reason for his presence at this gathering was because he had recently become engaged to Thelma, a fact that was to be publicly announced before the evening was out. How this hurried and altogether unsuitable engagement had come about, Thelma could never quite remember. But as far as Paul was concerned, it had definitely been a case of catching her on the rebound.

For years past, she had loved Robert. But Robert had turned out a failure, and after a great deal of deliberation she had decided to throw him over. This was the chance Paul had been waiting for. He stepped right in, taking Robert's place immediately, and at the same time exerted all the influence he had with her father. The scheme worked out even better than he could have expected, with the result that a few days after Thelma had broken with Robert, she was inveigled into an engagement to Paul.

He well knew that he owed a great deal of his success to the intercession of her father; knew also that she was still in her heart of hearts in love with Robert, and was only consenting to this out of a deep sense of filial duty. That counted as naught to him. He needed her, physically even more than mentally; so he was seizing his opportunity, and damning whatever consequences the immediate future might hold in store for him. Being tremendously proud of his victory, he was feeling irritated in no small degree by the promise he had made to hold his peace until her father arrived to make the announcement.

Benjamin's brother Isador, a rabbi, was holding forth at great length, concerning what he called the cowardice of Joan Dycer, the woman who had committed suicide.

'Any man or woman who takes his own life is guilty of treachery to God, and a weak and cowardly inability to face the facts of life.' With these words, he brought his lengthy dissertation to a close. Folding his arms, he sat back, obviously waiting for somebody to contradict him. As one might have expected, the one to do so was Paul.

'But my dear Mr. Fredericks,' he began with his irritating drawl, 'what you have just said is merely a contradiction in terms. You tell us at the beginning that the person committing suicide will receive a punishment in the next world far heavier than any they could be condemned to in this. Then, having admitted so much, you still persist in calling them cowards; whereas by your own showing, the fact that they are willing to face all this proves just the opposite.'

'No, it does not,' the old man retorted hotly, 'for they are people who don't believe in the penalty to come. They are people with no faith, no principles — '

'Oh, come, isn't that a little hard?' Thelma's voice was as sweet and gentle as her appearance.

'In other words, none of them are

42

spiritualists, I suppose?' Paul chimed in with a sneer.

'Quite so,' Isador replied with dignity. 'No good spiritualist would take his own life.'

'I wonder.'

The sneer in Paul's voice was so pronounced that Thelma looked in his direction with a slight frown.

'I don't think one can generalise about such things.' The softly spoken words came from a little figure seated well back from the fireplace. The speaker, like his voice, was quiet and retiring. His name was Doctor Prescott, and he was one of Benjamin's oldest friends.

'That's right, Doctor,' returned Thelma with a smile. 'Circumstances alter cases, don't they?'

'I quite agree, my dear.'

The little old man, himself the very spirit of tolerance, murmured these last words as though in fear of another onslaught from Isador.

'Possibly,' Isador assented graciously. 'But we can be too tolerant. In fact, it's a growing habit these days to make excuses for everything. For some things there are no excuses whatsoever.'

'And you think suicide's one of them, Uncle?' Thelma inquired.

Isador nodded his head definitely. For him, the discussion was at an end.

But Paul wouldn't let it rest there. 'What does Tony think about it?' he demanded abruptly. 'Come on, Tony! Give us your considered opinion on the subject.'

'I never take sides,' Tony Hargraves murmured from the depths of his arm-chair. Thus spoke Virginia's fiancé.

'Oh, come on, Tony, that's not fair,' Thelma put in, covering her irritation with a smile.

'No. I never allow myself to be drawn into other people's discussions,' Tony declared solemnly, and immediately relapsed into his former attitude of drowsy boredom.

Paul laughed, while the two older men looked rather surprised but made no comment.

Really, Thelma thought to herself, *I can't think what Virginia can see in such a dull young man.* She glanced over his good-looking face and slim figure. *He's all right to look at,* she mused, *but he always seems so bored with everybody.* And looking away from him, she was forced to the same conclusion she had arrived at so many times before; namely that no mere spectator can ever judge what people in love see in each other. Why, who would have thought that she and Robert — ? But that was a thought she must fight against. She must try to put him right out of her mind.

She had to see him over the weekend, as he'd been invited to the party by her father, who had not consulted her. But directly that was over she must cut him right out: she would be engaged to Paul then, and it wouldn't be fair to him if she went on seeing Robert. And then, last but not least, there were her father's wishes to be considered — she always thought of him as her father, rather than step-father, because he had done so much for her. He had never liked Robert very much, although he had done his best to be polite to him, for her sake. But Paul he did like, and therefore she felt it her bounden duty to stand by her decision to marry him, however hard it might be.

So thus she argued with herself, wrestling with her desires, in a strong determination to kill her love for a man she deemed already lost beyond all hope. It was a losing battle from the beginning, although in her blindness she refused to see it.

Suddenly silence fell upon them, rendering it possible for Thelma to overhear voices and footsteps out in the hall that would have otherwise passed unnoticed. Glad of any excuse, she jumped up; and, explaining that she was just going to see if her father had returned, ran out of the room.

But it was Virginia, and not her father, whom she found in the hall. A Virginia surprisingly pale and haggard. She turned to Thelma and said in a dull, tired voice, 'I've just been telling Parker I'm going to lie down for a bit.'

'Oh dear, aren't you well?' Her sister's pallor had genuinely alarmed Thelma.

'I'm all right,' Virginia replied in the same harsh tone. 'A bit tired, that's all.'

'Won't you be coming in to dinner,

dear? Father'll be so disappointed if you don't.'

'Sorry, but I can't help that. Explain it to him, will you?' She turned towards the staircase.

'Of course,' Thelma replied. Then, as the thought struck her, 'Would you like to have your dinner sent up to you?'

'No, thanks,' Virginia snapped out as she slowly mounted the stairs. 'And if I don't come down at all, you'll know I've gone to bed. See nobody disturbs me, will you?'

'Very well, dear.'

Thelma stood and watched her until she disappeared round the curve in the staircase. Frowning, she turned back towards the lounge. She'd never seen Virginia like this before; that ghostly pallor, and her hoarse voice. The fact that she'd retired to bed on her father's birthday — the only time during the whole year when she deigned to mix with the family . . . She'd never failed to be present. So it must be something very serious to make her do so now. For one moment, Thelma was on the point of going up to her room to see if she could be of any use to her. But she realised how useless it would be. They'd never visited each other's rooms in years; it would certainly look most strange if she began doing so now.

So with another baffled glance towards the staircase, she turned her steps once again in the direction of the lounge. As she did so, she thought of Tony, for whom, as she surmised, the past two hours had only been made bearable by the belief that he would soon be seeing his fiancée. Poor Tony! Thelma began to feel quite compassionate towards him. He certainly did wake up a bit when Virginia was around, and it was her secret belief that Virginia was the only one of them he cared about; she and her father evidently bored him. After all, there must be some explanation for his extraordinary conduct. He couldn't behave like that always, or he'd never be invited anywhere.

She shook her head. It was going to be difficult; she could feel it in her bones. Oh dear! If only Father . . .

There was a loud bang from the front

door, and she turned to see her step-father hurrying down the hall to meet her. 'Daddy!' She ran forward, throwing her arms around him and kissing him warmly. 'I was just hoping you'd come,' she cried joyously.

Benjamin Fredericks laughed his deep, sonorous laugh and kissed his pretty step-daughter tenderly. 'And why?' he inquired.

'Oh, lots of things.' She snuggled closer to him. 'One, all the guests are here, and I've had to entertain them.'

'Which I'm sure you've done far better than I could.'

'Anyway, it's time you came in and had a shot at it yourself. But what's made you so late, darling?'

'I had to talk over some business.'

'The usual businessman's excuse?' Thelma said with a provocative smile. 'But you are naughty, you know.'

'And I'm penitent. Now, what's the next tremendous worry on my little lady's mind?'

'Well,' she said slowly, her smile vanishing, 'it's Virginia.'

'Virginia?' Benjamin looked surprised.

'Yes. She came in just before you did, and behaved most strangely. She looked so odd. All pale and distracted. I don't know what to make of it.'

'Where is she now?'

'She's gone upstairs to her room.'

'Is she ill?'

'I don't know, but she asked not to be disturbed, and she also said she wouldn't be coming down to dinner.'

'Not coming down?' Benjamin seemed mystified.

'Yes, I know,' she replied, looking up at him. 'It surprised me too. And she said if she didn't put in an appearance at all, it meant she was asleep, and I must explain. But it's so awkward, isn't it?'

'Shall I see if there's anything I can do for her?' He made a slight movement towards the stairs.

'I shouldn't, dear,' said Thelma, catching him by the arm.

'Let her get over it herself? Well, perhaps you're right.'

'What I'm worried about is poor Tony.'

Benjamin smiled. 'He'll be like a fish

out of water if she's not there to look after him, won't he?'

'That's just what I'm afraid of. He's begun to already.' She started to help him out of his coat.

'You've no other surprises for me, have you?' he inquired as he handed his hat to Parker, who, like the perfect butler he was, always appeared when he was wanted.

'Yes, I have,' she declared in a definite tone. 'But I'm not sure if I ought to tell you . . . It's Uncle Isador. He's here. In the lounge.'

'Then he *has* come,' Benjamin declared, smiling.

Thelma's face dropped. 'You knew?'

'Yes, I knew,' he admitted. 'I asked him to come. But he wouldn't make up his mind till the last moment.'

'But why did you keep it a secret?'

'Because it was to be my surprise for you,' he said, taking her by the arm.

'I don't understand. How could you have asked him to come when you haven't seen each other for years?'

'I *have* seen him. I saw him yesterday.' He held her close. 'I met Isador one night, quite by accident, not having seen him for years. And it so happens that he's living only four miles from this very house.'

'So that's why you've been taking those midnight drives of yours?'

'Exactly. I've been going to Isador's nearly every night. But that's our secret, so don't forget it. And at last he's come here. Are you satisfied?'

Thelma nodded. 'There's still one thing I'd like you to tell me, though,' she said gravely. 'What was it you and Uncle Isador quarrelled about in the first place, that's kept you apart all this time?'

Benjamin led her firmly towards the lounge. 'That, my darling child, is too long a story to tell you now,' he said with a laugh.

And before she had time to question him further, they were in the lounge facing their guests, who rose at their entrance.

Benjamin at once advanced towards his brother. 'So you decided to come after all,' he said with genuine enthusiasm, and they shook hands.

Standing side by side, it was difficult to think of them as brothers; they were so dissimilar. Benjamin was the most striking of the two. Tall, slender, with iron-grey hair and bright intelligent eyes, he was a man whom one could never under any circumstances overlook. He was a great *presence*.

In physique, Isador was unlike his brother. He was small, with thick black hair and extraordinary little eyes like pinpoints. One could not detect the faintest glint of humour anywhere in the granite-hardness of his countenance. But Isador was also impressive in his own way, although the atmosphere with which he surrounded himself was a little less theatrical than that favoured by his brother.

Everybody had risen at Benjamin's entrance. The handshake between the two brothers only lasted for a few seconds, and immediately afterwards Benjamin was surrounded by his guests, whom he begged to forgive him for his late arrival. Such was his charm of manner that nobody could have felt annoyed with him, and conversation was just about to turn onto ordinary channels when Paul suddenly spoke in a tone that embarrassed and surprised all of them.

'Aren't you forgetting something, Mr. Fredericks?' he demanded suddenly.

Benjamin turned to him. 'I don't think so,' he said slowly. 'Why, do you remember something that I should have done?'

'Yes.' Paul's voice was uncompromising. 'Don't you think it's time to make that announcement, Mr. Fredericks?'

The silence grew more intense. The word 'announcement' had caught everybody's attention; all were looking towards Benjamin for his answer.

'It'll be better after dinner, Paul. Soon enough.' He turned towards the door, hoping to bluff it out. But it was no use.

'I think Thelma and I would prefer it now, if you don't mind, sir.'

Thelma looked surprised, never having expressed any wish. She could feel a flush mounting her cheeks. So the moment had come! When she had suddenly consented to become engaged to Paul, in a fit of pique, she had never realised how determined he was. She was only just beginning to feel his strength at this moment, and she wasn't liking it. She found herself resenting his air of mastery and the cold, dogged way in which he was commanding her father to announce their engagement now, instead of waiting until later in the evening. There was something definitely unpleasant about it.

In the distance, the front doorbell clanged. But nobody noticed it. They were all too engrossed in what was about to happen.

'Yes, Father,' Thelma said in a low voice. 'I wish it.'

Seeing he had no choice, Benjamin began to announce in a quiet voice the engagement of his step-daughter Thelma to Mr. Paul Conway. He said it all simply and unaffectedly, letting a sigh of relief escape him at the finish.

This over, the first to congratulate the engaged couple was Tony; for a few seconds he seemed quite brilliantly awake. His first remark, not in the best of taste, was a loud 'Gawd blimey!' directly Benjamin had finished speaking. But he apologised for this immediately afterwards and made amends nobly by congratulating them in an unexpectedly charming manner. After which, he relapsed once more into his usual torpor.

Then they were suitably congratulated by Isador — a little prosily perhaps — and finally by Doctor Prescott. But to Thelma there was still one voice missing. The voice which, although she wouldn't have dared to admit it at that moment, in reality meant more to her than all the others put together, including her fiancé's.

That voice, however, was not missing for long. 'Congratulations,' came in hollow tones from the end of the room.

Standing in the open doorway, swaying slightly to and fro, was Robert!

4

A Doomed Man

He advanced slowly into the room; on closer inspection, he proved to be less intoxicated than his first appearance might have led one to believe. Standing face to face with Thelma, he proffered her his hand. She took it timidly.

'Congratulations,' he repeated. 'I hope you'll be very happy.'

'I hope so too,' she said. Smiling, she added, 'but it'll be time enough to wish us that when we're married.'

'I prefer to do it now,' he said solemnly. 'Who knows? I might not be here then.'

She took a step backwards. There was a prophetic ring about that last sentence that had struck her to the heart.

Benjamin patted him on the shoulder. 'Don't say that, old man,' he said with a kindly smile. 'You'll be here all right.'

'Who knows?' Robert spoke in the

same faraway voice. There was something uncanny about it — everybody felt it this time. He was a different man to the Robert Thelma had known. Something had changed him entirely. He was doomed, she told herself. A doomed man! Somehow that description seemed to fit him. Very dimly, she heard her father introducing him to Isador. And they all began to drift back to their seats by the fire. But she still remained standing.

It was some queer quality about the expression in his eyes that was so fascinating to her; like a rather terrifying vacuum. She felt she wanted to take him into her arms; to tell him she'd only become engaged to Paul because she'd lost her temper with him; to tell him how much she really loved him — anything in her power to soothe away that terrible hurt she knew she had inflicted upon him, and which he was now trying to disguise from her.

'Come and sit by the fire, Thelma. You'll get cold out there.'

It was Benjamin's voice. Mechanically she obeyed him, and seated herself in her armchair by the fireplace. She felt a hand creeping over hers. Looking up, she saw Paul smiling at her, and with a great effort she smiled back.

Robert was sitting opposite her, gazing into the flames. She noticed that he was faultlessly dressed in tails; an outfit ill-becoming the grim set of his features. Benjamin rose to his feet.

'And now if you'll all excuse me, I really must go and change. Look after them while I'm gone, Thelma dear.'

'All right, Father.'

With a last cheery nod to his guests, Benjamin went out.

Thelma made a conscientious effort to rouse herself. Somehow she had never felt less like entertaining people in her life. Something inside her seemed to have snapped.

She looked round the room. At the far end the two old gentlemen were talking quietly, while Tony was again falling off to sleep. 'Tony!' she called sharply. 'Don't go to sleep!'

'Sorry,' he apologised. 'It's waiting for Virginia that's making me sleepy. How much longer is she going to be?'

'I'm afraid she's been back some time, Tony,' Thelma explained. 'I meant to tell you, only Robert turning up so suddenly put it right out of my head.'

'Did you say she'd been here some time?' Tony demanded incredulously. 'Isn't she coming down to dinner?'

'She came in just before Daddy, and said she was going to lie down. But she said she might come down later — '

A smile appeared on Tony's face instantly.

'She didn't guarantee it, though,' she hastened to add. 'It all depends on whether she gets to sleep or not.'

Tony sank back into his chair again, his mind once more completely at rest.

'Is this Virginia you were talking about, my dear?' inquired Doctor Prescott during a momentary pause in his conversation with Isador.

'Yes, Doctor. She was feeling very tired.'

'I'm sorry. I should like to have seen her,' said Isador.

'I think you'd like her,' Paul said. But

from his manner of speaking, it was quite evident that there was no love lost between him and Virginia.

Robert remained silent.

'Oh, by the way, Thelma,' Doctor Prescott went on, 'Mr. Fredericks and I have been having a most interesting discussion about billiards. We find we're both great enthusiasts. Has Benjamin, by any chance, still got that splendid table of his in use?'

'Indeed he has, Doctor,' Thelma replied.

'Do you think we might have time for a game before dinner?'

'Of course,' she said, nodding. 'Tony, would you show Uncle Isador and Doctor Prescott to the billiard room for me?'

He rose heavily to his feet, moving towards the door. 'This way, gentlemen. Will you let me score for you?'

The two men expressed their delight at this unexpected offer as they followed him from the room. Thelma's glance wandered again in the direction of Robert. But still he neither moved nor spoke.

Paul patted her affectionately. She noticed that nasty, possessive smile again hovering at the corners of his lips, and all at once experienced a great feeling of revulsion, a desire to rush from the room.

'You're not going to leave us, are you, dear?' His voice was as suave and silken as his smile.

'I — I must go and see how they're getting on in the kitchen,' she stammered, beginning to panic. 'I shan't be long.' She turned and fled.

Paul rose and stood looking after her. So she wanted to run away, did she? That was something new. 'I wonder why she did that,' he said aloud, forgetting Robert was still in the room with him.

'Did what?' Robert looked up at him. His voice sounded strained.

'Oh, nothing,' he said lightly, endeavouring to pass it off. 'It only seemed to me as though she was running away from us.'

Running away from *us*! The sentence kept repeating itself in Robert's ear. Or had she only been running away from one of them? Was she was running away from him? Since he had walked in those few moments previously and heard her engagement announced to Paul, anything seemed possible, and even likely. But still he found it difficult to believe. For though Thelma had thrown him over, the last thing in the world he had expected was for her to get engaged again so soon. It seemed incredible that she could have recovered from it so quickly.

Maybe she hadn't? Supposing it were just a blind, to show him how well she could get on without him? But if that were the case, it seemed a bit far to go to all the trouble of an engagement. Of course, she could break it off; but it wasn't like Thelma to play such a shabby trick on Paul. She might have started out with the objective of giving him a lesson, but now that it had gone as far as this, he knew it would have to be something pretty serious that could prevent her from carrying her project through to the finish.

And, worst of all, the whole thing had been his own fault! There he had been, with Thelma madly in love with him and ready to do anything in her power to help him, and all he'd done was to throw it into the gutter. He refused to interest himself in anything; to moderate his drinking, or to give up the useless set to which he belonged. Thelma had become fed up. She'd tried her best and failed. He was useless to himself and to her; so doing the only thing left in her power she returned his engagement ring, and made up her mind to put him right out of her life for ever.

'Have a whisky and soda?' Paul broke in upon his unpleasant reflections.

'Thanks.'

I hope she'll be happy, anyway, he thought to himself, *for if anyone deserves happiness, it's Thelma.*

He looked towards Paul's back as he poured out the drinks. Perhaps he'd been mistaken in him, and it was just his manner that was unfortunate. After all, he'd only known him for about six weeks. But on the other hand, Thelma had only known him a little over six weeks too.

Paul handed him his drink. 'Take this, old man. It'll make you feel better.'

'I'm all right,' Robert said. 'Just a bit

sleepy, that's all.'

Paul raised his glass. 'To Thelma!' he said with ill-concealed triumph.

Robert looked at him in surprise. That note of conquest had not escaped him; nor had it pleased him. He found his dislike of Paul steadily increasing. 'To Thelma!' he repeated quietly.

They drank for a few moments in silence.

'Awfully good of you to take it like this, Robert,' Paul said with the same air of patronage. 'My engagement to Thelma and all that.'

'I hadn't much choice, had I?'

'I don't know. You could have been very unpleasant about it just now, if you'd chosen to make a scene.'

'And what use would that have been?'

'Oh, no use at all. Still, you might have tried it.'

'You didn't take long to fill my place, did you?'

Paul gave an uneasy laugh. 'All's fair in love and war, you know.'

'Exactly. But one doesn't refer to it afterwards.' Robert's last words were shot out with biting sarcasm.

'I'm sorry. I didn't know you felt it as strongly as that.'

'Well, I do. So we'll let the matter drop.' Robert hastily swallowed off what was left of his drink.

Taking his glass from him, Paul placed it along with his own on the cabinet. 'Cigarette?' He opened his case and offered him one.

'No, thanks.'

Robert watched him as he took one himself and lit it. His wave of self-abasement was passing, its place being taken by one of dull resentment. What was there about Paul that made him such a desirable match for Thelma? Nothing, so far as they knew. The only person likely to have any knowledge of him was Benjamin, and he seemed to like him for some reason. Although even he had appeared a little unwilling to announce the engagement until he had been forced into it.

Stretching himself out in one of the armchairs, Paul leant back luxuriously. 'I gather the old man celebrates his birthday like this every year,' he remarked, as though trying to make conversation.

'Yes,' Robert answered without looking at him. 'Of course, this is the first time you've been, isn't it?'

'To one of his parties? Yes. How many have you been to?'

'This is my third.' For three years he'd been madly in love with Thelma. She'd certainly given him a long run.

'I suppose they're all right, really. Only, it always seems rather pathetic to me for a man of that age to be thinking of birthday parties.'

'Why?' Robert's voice was beginning to have a distinctly hostile ring in it.

'Well, he's sixty, you know. I thought most people of that age liked to tactfully overlook their birthdays.'

'Well, Mr. Fredericks doesn't. He's the kind of man who doesn't try to overlook anything. He's straightforward with himself, which is more than some people I know. And if he chooses to enjoy his birthday by having his friends around him, why shouldn't he?'

'No reason at all, old man. It seems a

little silly, that's all.'

'Silly!' Robert turned away with an expression of disgust. This man was goading him too far, confound him. Why should he be so superior about everything? Even about the father of the woman he hoped to marry? 'You'd better not say that to Thelma or you'll never hear the end of it,' he remarked.

'Why not?' Paul gave a supercilious smirk. 'I expect she thinks it's as stupid as I do.'

'She doesn't. Thelma adores her step-father.'

'That's no reason why she shouldn't see his faults.'

'Well, I'm warning you.'

Paul slowly exhaled a cloud of smoke. 'Thanks, but I don't think it'll be necessary.'

The two men relapsed into silence. After a few seconds, Robert began to fidget. Though he'd recovered from his drunkenness, his head still felt extraordinarily woolly, and it was all he could do to think coherently, for his mind was shadowed with memories of things

— several of them unpleasant — which had taken place during the day. He rose to his feet.

'I think I'll have a look at my room if you don't mind,' he said by way of an excuse, and began to walk towards the door.

'Don't let me drive you away, old chap,' came from the armchair by the fireplace. 'I've quite enjoyed our little talk together — honestly I have.'

'I'm glad,' Robert said shortly, and stretched out his hand towards the handle.

'Then come and talk some more. There's plenty of time to look at your room after dinner.'

'I think I'd rather see it now, thank you.'

'Very well. Sorry if I scare you.'

Robert had the door partly open, but paused; and closing it, hurriedly came back to face his tormentor. 'Why should I be frightened of you?' he demanded, towering over him threateningly.

Paul looked up with feigned surprise. 'How should I know? Unless it's that you're afraid you might lose your temper with me?'

'And so ruin myself even more completely in Thelma's eyes? Oh no, Paul! I wouldn't do that. You're not worth it!'

'Thank you.' The insult seemed to pass him by unnoticed, and he went on as offensively as before. 'Don't forget, though, that I'm your rival, will you? Your successful rival, I might add.'

It was Robert's turn to sneer now. His lip curled contemptuously. 'That, my dear Paul, was a freak of nature I can never hope to understand.'

'I don't expect you to,' the other retorted coolly. 'It was really quite easy, though. Taking your place called for neither skill nor finesse; it was a walkover.'

'You swine!'

'There you are! Losing your temper already. You asked for the truth and you've got it. Thelma was only too glad to be rid of you. Otherwise, how could I have got away with it so quickly?'

'It's a damned lie!'

'Very well, just as you please. Perhaps you'd better go and look at your room after all, before you lose control of yourself altogether.'

Robert's thin margin of control was rapidly giving way. For once, Paul's sense of timing a situation had played him false. This time he had gone too far. Without the least warning, he found himself seized roughly by the throat and pulled to his feet. Facing him were the glaring eyes and furious features of Robert.

'You'll apologise for that,' he cried hoarsely.

Paul felt his legs beginning to shake beneath him, but made one last effort to keep up a bold front. 'I'll see you in hell first.'

'By God, I'll — '

The grip on his throat tightened, while a feeling as of paralysis began to creep over his whole body. He tried to raise his hands, but they seemed to be fixed to his sides with weights of lead. Everything started to go dark before his eyes. All he could see were two wild, glaring orbs . . .

Then something happened! He heard

voices — at first in the far distance; but they soon grew closer. Then the deathlike grip on his throat was hastily withdrawn; and with a gasp of relief he sank back into the armchair.

For a few minutes he didn't dare open his eyes. All he did was to draw in long painful breaths, which grew slowly easier as the time passed. When he did finally open them, however, it was to see Thelma bending over him, and to note with pleasure the look of genuine anxiety upon her face and the cool touch of her hand against his throbbing brow.

'Are you all right?'

'Yes, thanks!' He smiled with an effort. 'Just trying — to get my — breath back — that's all.'

His glance wandered round the room. He saw Benjamin (now changed for dinner) standing just behind Thelma, looking at him anxiously; and at some little distance, leaning against the mantelpiece, with his head buried in his hands, was Robert. Not a sound came from him. He was like a figure cast in stone.

Paul closed his eyes with a smile of

contentment. Now was his chance to be magnanimous and play the hero. He'd never dreamed Robert would lose his temper as easily as that, or he wouldn't have dared to have gone so far. But perhaps it was all for the best. Robert was in disgrace, and would not dare disclose the cause of their quarrel. That made him the injured party and therefore entitled to all the sympathy Thelma and her father could give him.

His mind made up he opened his eyes again. 'I'm much better now,' he said weakly. 'If you'll help me, dear, I'll come along into dinner.'

'Of course.' Thelma slipped her arm under his with prompt alacrity.

'Allow me to help you too,' said Benjamin, coming to his other side and doing likewise. Together they assisted him to rise.

But the moment he reached an upright, posture he turned deathly white. This was no trickery on his part, for Robert had really displayed superhuman strength in those few seconds during which he had had him at his mercy. Besides which, Paul was anything but an outstandingly strong man.

'Sure you're all right?' Benjamin enquired nervously as he perceived the change in him.

'In a minute . . . ' He braced himself, looking straight ahead of him. In a few minutes he felt better. He nodded to Thelma with a smile.

'I'm quite all right, now,' he said.

'And may I enquire what it was all about?' asked Benjamin, throwing a sidelong glance towards Robert.

'If you'll forgive me, Mr. Fredericks,' said Paul with dignity, 'I'd rather let it drop altogether.'

'Well, of course, just as you please,' Benjamin answered gruffly. 'But it's a most unusual thing to happen, and I should have thought — '

'Let it drop, Father dear,' Thelma urged.

'Very well. Just as you say.'

Paul turned to him as one about to deliver himself of a great and noble confidence. 'That's very kind of you, sir,' he said with a grateful smile. 'I'm afraid

Mr. Harcourt rather forgot himself just now, and — well, I think it's best for all of us if we let it go at that.'

'You mean it's best for Mr. Harcourt if we let it go at that.' It was Thelma's voice that spoke, and it sounded unexpectedly on the verge of tears.

'Best for both of us,' he hastened to assure her.

'You're being a lot kinder to him than he deserves,' she continued in a quavering tone. 'He's disgraced himself. A great many people would have had him up for assault!'

'Oh, no. Nothing as bad as that.'

'I must say you're being very lenient with him, Paul,' declared Benjamin, in agreement with his step-daughter.

The object of his praise smiled wistfully. 'Well, we couldn't allow anything to upset your birthday party, could we, sir?' he said with a touch of hypocrisy. 'Why, it would spoil everything if this came out. So I suggest we go on as though nothing had happened. And when he's sufficiently recovered, Robert had better come in to dinner too. Then nobody will be any the wiser. Don't you agree?'

Benjamin nodded his head in approbation, although obviously still dying with curiosity as to the cause of the whole thing; and the three of them began to walk slowly towards the door. After a few paces they stopped, and Thelma turned back to Robert, who was still standing by the mantelpiece.

'At least,' she said defiantly, 'I think you owe Paul an apology.'

But not a syllable did he speak, nor by the flicker of a muscle did he alter his position.

Paul gently disengaged himself from his two companions and moved towards the door. Dutifully Thelma ran ahead and opened it for him, then stood aside while he walked slowly out, followed by Benjamin. Just about to do the same herself, she was seized by a sudden impulse and turned back once again towards Robert.

'You weren't even man enough to apologise,' she said in a hoarse whisper. Tears were now coursing down her cheeks, and an expression of horror had begun to cross her face. 'You looked as though you could have murdered him!' she added. And with a little cry, she ran from the room.

Robert raised his head in silence; turned in the direction she had gone. His hands were clutched convulsively, his face distorted into a dreadful leer.

'Murder'! The word crashed in his ears like a peal of thunder. He looked at his watch. Eight o'clock. In four hours' time! The words of the fortune teller came back to him . . . 'As the clock strikes the hour of midnight . . . you will become a murderer!'

Four hours to wait! He clapped his hands against his mouth to choke back the wild laugh that arose, unbidden, to his lips!

5

The Victim

Dinner, in spite of Benjamin's best efforts, was rather embarrassing. To begin with, Robert's appearance about ten minutes after the meal had begun struck a peculiar note, for he never said more than about two sentences during the whole time, and made no attempt to excuse his lateness at all. Thelma had obviously been crying, and Paul ate sparingly, and looked as white as death. All these circumstances together were too much to be overlooked, even by such an absent-minded old gentleman as Doctor Prescott, and were promptly noted down by the meticulous Isador. However, as good breeding demanded, no questions were asked, and they were each allowed to keep their own little secrets.

In spite even of Benjamin's well-phrased toast to the engaged couple, it was not until they had returned to the lounge for coffee that things began to brighten up. The pleasant hum of conversation started slowly growing louder, and the atmosphere of a jolly English weekend party began to prevail at last.

Robert had retired to his room immediately after dinner, on some pretext or other. Thelma was valiantly endeavouring to carry on a conversation with Tony, while Isador had returned to an interminable argument on the pros and cons of spiritualism with Paul.

Hence it came about that Doctor Prescott had ample opportunity for his conversation with Benjamin. 'Can I have a few words with you, Benjamin?' he asked in his soft voice.

'Of course you can,' Benjamin said warmly. 'I haven't seen anything of you all the evening. What have you been doing with yourself?'

'I'm afraid I've been rather monopolised — if I may venture to use the term — by your brother. You see — '

'I know — billiards and spiritualism. Both rather heavy topics. So you hope to get a little relaxation by talking to me? Well, what do you want to talk about, eh?'

'I'm afraid it's something rather serious, Benjamin. I hope it isn't the wrong time to introduce such a topic, but I — ' The old man trailed away into incoherence.

'Come and sit over here, where we shan't be disturbed, and tell me all about it.' Benjamin drew the doctor towards the window seat, far out of earshot of the rest of the party.

After clearing his throat, the doctor plunged in and bluntly proffered the information he had been keeping back until such a suitable moment should arrive. 'It's about that interview we had last week. Since then, I've given the matter a great deal of thought.'

'You mean you've given my case a great deal of thought?'

'Yes. Your case. I've been over all you told me, and your symptoms, together with the results of my examination. And it all confirms my first impression — about your heart.'

'Well, you've already told me that,

Doctor. You said my heart wasn't too strong and I should have to take good care of it. That was all you said, as far as I remember.'

'Yes. That was all I said — then. But I should have said that my deductions strengthened my first impression.'

'You mean that my heart's worse than you thought then?'

'Much worse,' Doctor Prescott said solemnly.

'But this is dreadful, Doctor.'

The doctor hastened to reassure him. 'Come now, you mustn't look upon the black side of things. But on the other hand, with an energetic nature like yours, unless you realise the full seriousness of it all, you might quite easily overstep your strength. That's why I've told you. If you'd been an ordinary placid sort of man who led a dull, unemotional life, I should have thought twice before telling you. But you're not. I've not known you for all these years without discovering that.'

'I see. Thank you, Doctor.' Benjamin's voice was quiet; he had received a great shock.

He was casting his mind back over the events that had led up to his sudden decision to visit Doctor Prescott in his professional capacity in town. It had all begun about a couple of years ago, when he had become suddenly conscious of acute pains in the region of his heart. As time went on, and they came and went, he found all sorts of explanations to account for them. Indigestion was the one that convinced him the most. Or he'd tell himself it was because he was overtired or run down, or it was rheumatism. Always he had some new excuse. When he was in pain, he vowed to go to the doctor the next day. But when the next day arrived and the pain had gone, the decision to go to the doctor went also.

It was not until one night a little over a week ago, after suffering an unusually violent attack of this pain, that he actually brought himself to ring up Doctor Prescott and arrange for an appointment the following day. When the interview took place, Doctor Prescott was by turns sceptical, interested, and finally seriously alarmed.

Smiling kindly, he continued in the voice that had made him so beloved to all his patients: 'Be careful, that's all. Don't get excited or rush about or — '

'It may prove fatal. That's what you were going to say, wasn't it?'

'Well, serious, let us say. But there, I'm sure you'll be careful, now that I've told you all about it, won't you? Just see that you don't overdo it.'

'I will.'

'Good.' The old man smiled delightedly. 'And no nocturnal drives, either. Isador's just been telling me how you've been visiting him three or four times every week in the early hour of the morning to bring about this reconciliation. He says you did it so as to give the women a big surprise. Is that true?'

'It is. And I've done it. I've affected the reconciliation and the women have had their big surprise. Now everybody's contented.'

'So there'll be no need for any more of those midnight rides?' the doctor persisted doggedly.

'Why should there be? It's all over.'

'Well, I'm glad of that,' the old man said fervently. 'It's always tempting providence when a man of your age starts gallivanting about, you know.'

'Thanks all the same for your advice, Doctor,' Benjamin said sincerely. 'I'll do just as you say. But I want you to promise me you won't tell Thelma anything about all this. You see, she didn't even know I'd been to see you. And I don't want her worried at all; she's too young and sweet.

'I promise.'

'Thank you.' Benjamin's voice sounded genuinely grateful as he patted the older man's shoulder.

As he said this, Paul, excusing himself from his conversation with Isador, came across to them and addressed himself to Benjamin, apparently oblivious to the doctor's presence. 'I want to thank you for your good wishes, sir,' he began with a smile intended to be disarming.

'Not at all, Paul. Least I could do.'

'And I'd like to thank you also,' Paul continued, 'for announcing the engagement before dinner, as I asked you to, instead of after. I was afraid you must have thought me a little aggressive about it.'

'No, I didn't. I understood, perfectly.'

'It was just excitement, that's all. You don't get engaged to a beautiful woman like Thelma every day, so you can't blame me for being excited, can you?'

'I don't blame you. Who said I did?'

Paul dropped his eyes as though embarrassed. 'Nobody. Only I was afraid you might. Or even that Thelma might herself.'

'Surely Thelma's the last person who should take offence at your impatience? It was a compliment to her.'

'Of course it was. But if she mentions it, I'd be awfully glad if you'd explain it to her as best you can. Will you?'

Benjamin laughed. 'Of course.'

This was Paul in a very different guise — trying to be polite! That certainly was a departure. Paul smiled and held out his hand. Benjamin took it. 'Now go ahead and enjoy yourself, my boy.'

'You bet I will.'

'It's a very comfortable house, young man, isn't it?' the doctor put in, determined not to be ignored completely.

'It certainly is,' Paul replied heartily. Then he stopped himself. 'Except for one thing,' he added. 'My bedroom's full of the most curious noises. I'm sorry to say they woke me up once or twice.'

'Why didn't you tell me this before?' Benjamin sounded a little grieved. Although one of the nouveau riche himself, he was a naturally good host, and this sudden piece of information concerning the discomfort of a guest rather upset him.

'I didn't like to.'

'I wish you had. I don't like to think of any of my guests being uncomfortable. What are you next to?'

'Virginia's room, on one side.'

'That's the room with the communicating door, isn't it?'

'Yes, that's right.'

'Then on the other you must be up against the bathroom. It's possibly the pipes or something.'

'Very likely. You see, I'd never slept there before until last night. But don't worry about it. It's not as bad as all that. I expect I'll get used to it in time.' And with a wave of his hand, he walked away to join Thelma.

The impression he left behind him was a distinctly unpleasant one. He had started off by being unusually polite. But this complaint about his bedroom was a direct return to the aggressive manner he had assumed towards Benjamin concerning the announcement before dinner.

'What can Benjamin see in the boy?' the doctor kept asking himself. 'He's not good-looking or even civil, and money can obviously be no object.'

'He's a strange boy, that Paul,' he said, putting his thoughts into words.

Benjamin nodded. 'It's his manner, that's all. He's a good lad, really, Doctor. You can take it from me.'

Doctor Prescott shrugged. 'Well, you know best, I suppose.'

'I'm sorry about his bedroom, though,' Benjamin said slowly. 'I must see what I can do about that.'

'Give him mine,' said the little doctor promptly. 'I'm slightly deaf, so I shan't hear the old water pipes, or whatever it is.'

Benjamin laughed. 'Why, you're no

more deaf than I am.'

'Let that be as it may. I can stand a bad night's rest far better than you.'

'Stop talking about me as though I were a confirmed invalid,' Benjamin retorted with just a trace of irritation. 'We'll see what we can do about it.'

'That means you'll give up your room to him.'

'No it doesn't, not necessarily. Of course, if there's nobody else . . . However, it won't be yours. So now you know.'

'I think you're being very foolish, Benjamin. If you ask me, I think that boy's better fitted for it than either of us.'

'Possibly. But he's a guest, and he must be made comfortable.'

'I see.' He relapsed into a moody silence.

'Virginia!' This exclamation came from Thelma, and drew everybody's attention towards the doorway through which Virginia was just entering. Walking to the centre of the room, she confronted them, a determined smile upon her lips.

'I must apologise to you all for not coming down before,' she said in a steady voice, 'but I haven't been feeling very well. I hope you'll excuse me.'

Looking as she did at that moment, it would have been practically impossible to refuse her anything. She remained motionless, a dignified and altogether self-possessed figure.

The first person to open his mouth was Tony. He rose to his feet. He seemed to have been unexpectedly galvanised into action. His whole face came suddenly to life. Gone was the bored and indolent young figure of a few seconds ago. He came towards her and took her hands. 'I'll say we will,' he cried joyfully. 'Gosh, but it's good to see you.'

Virginia laughed, and for an instant her expression became a happy one.

'Are you sure you're all right, Virginia?' her father asked.

She turned to him, that peculiarly determined look on her face becoming even more marked. 'Well enough not to miss your birthday party. Does that satisfy you?' she said.

'I'm honoured,' her father said in a tone meant to be bantering, but in reality was remarkably genuine.

Paul shook her by the hand. 'Congratulations on your recovery,' he said facetiously.

But Virginia and Tony were apparently far too interested in one another to notice him. After a friendly nod to Doctor Prescott, they were just about to retire to the far end of the room when Benjamin stepped forward to stop them.

'Haven't you overlooked somebody?' he said, addressing himself to Virginia. 'Your Uncle Isador.'

Isador rose from his chair with a friendly smile and came towards her. Impulsively she held out her hand. 'How can you forgive me?' she murmured. 'And after all these years.'

He took her hand and pressed it warmly. Thus they stood looking into each other's eyes. Here were two people capable of being the best of friends, should circumstances permit. The family resemblance between them was strong; more in the expression than in actual features. They both possessed the same hard exteriors, but in both of them one could occasionally glimpse the softness underneath. And the smiles which shone on their faces at this moment were silently eloquent of the hidden charm of their characters.

'I've been looking forward to this moment for a long time,' he said to her in a low, well-modulated voice. 'I knew your mother well, my dear.'

'My mother?' Virginia's whole countenance expressed delighted surprise. Never before had she been spoken to like this. She smiled at him — a sweet friendly smile, which only very few were ever privileged to see.

'She was a great friend of mine.' Something suspiciously like moisture glistened in his eyes. It did not escape Virginia's notice.

'Do you know,' she said, 'you're the first person who's ever mentioned my mother to me.'

He slipped his arm lightly around her. 'Come and sit down, and let me tell you more.' He drew her gently towards the armchair he had just vacated, while poor Tony drifted disconsolately back towards Thelma.

Never could Virginia recall in the whole

course of her life such a delightful surprise as this unexpected meeting with Isador. His gentleness, the interest he had immediately shown in her, and the charming manner he had employed in speaking of her mother — whom she could barely call to mind — were all to be remembered by her for many a year to come.

'You were in love with my mother, weren't you?' she asked him as soon as the conversation around them had grown sufficiently loud to prevent any chances of their being overheard.

'How did you know?'

'I found some letters you had written her. She always kept them. I've kept them to this very day.'

'May I see them?'

'Of course. You don't want to now, do you?'

'Not now. Next time we meet. We're going to be great friends, aren't we?'

'You're the only friend I've got,' she answered simply.

'What about the young man?'

'Tony's not a friend, Uncle. I love him.'

He looked at her curiously. 'Are you sure, my dear?'

'Quite sure. I'll tell you why someday, when we've seen more of each other.'

'What does your father think about it?'

'The same as you. He can't understand it.'

Isador bowed his head. 'I'm afraid I can't.'

The woman at his side looked at him with great serious eyes. 'Then I'll tell you. He's the only person who's ever made me the least bit happy. He's the only person who tries to understand me. The only one who wants to understand me.'

'Don't say that.'

'Until now.' She pressed his hand again. 'So I've a great deal to thank him for.'

'I expect he's a great deal to thank you for, too.'

'Not so much.'

There was a pause while they gazed into the fire, but it was fraught with understanding. The kind of silence which can only exist between two people who are in perfect harmony with one another.

At last Virginia turned to him, and with an air of completely changing the subject, said, 'Tell me about my mother. I remember so little about her. What was she like? Was she tall? Fair?'

'No. Small and dark.'

'Pretty?'

'I thought so.'

He had given all his answers in a tone of deep respect, as though he were talking of something too beautiful to be described in words. Now he gave a sigh.

'Don't you think perhaps it would be better if we discussed this later, when we've seen more of each other?'

'All right.' Her voice was full of sympathy. 'I won't mention it again, until you give me leave.'

'Thank you. Is there anything else besides that you would like to know?'

She thought a second; then: 'What made you come here tonight?'

'Your father persuaded me.'

'Why didn't you come before, though?'

'Because — your father and I had a quarrel, many years ago, and we'd not seen each other for a long time.'

'I understand. You see, Uncle, that's in the letters too.'

'I might have known it. How pleased she would have been to know we'd made it up.'

'I'm pleased too.'

'It was your father's surprise for you.'

'Has it satisfied you?'

This question was addressed by Benjamin, who happened to have overheard Isador's last remark on his way across the room to get himself another whisky and soda.

'You bet it has.'

The three of them laughed contentedly. It was to the sound of this laughter that Robert quietly opened the door and slipped unobserved into the room. He stood gazing at them all, that glazed, uncomprehending look still in his eyes. Nobody seemed to know he was there; and he, for his own part, seemed loath to obtrude himself.

Virginia's laugh ended abruptly. 'Oh, Father! I'm so sorry! Your birthday present — I forgot to bring it back from town!'

'You forgot?'

'Yes. You know, the cigarette case I promised to give you?'

'I thought you'd changed your mind. When I went up to dress for dinner I found a little present on my dressing-table, and I took it for granted that it came from you.'

'Wasn't there any note with it?'

'No. I looked most carefully.'

'How strange.'

'Why didn't you mention this before, Father?' asked Thelma, catching the tail end of the discussion.

All other conversation had ceased, and the whole room was concentrated upon Benjamin's words. 'Well, because of that little trouble we had before dinner, dear,' he explained with slight embarrassment. 'It put it right out of my mind.'

'Where is it?' Virginia asked curiously.

'In my pocket.' He put his hand into his pocket and presently withdrew a little box. Opening it, he took out a small, bright object that he held up to the light.

'How beautiful!' This exclamation came from both women simultaneously. Even

96

Tony sat up and blinked.

'What is it?' he said stupidly, gazing at the glittering circle between Benjamin's finger and thumb.

'A ring,' came the reply. 'I should say it must be a genuine diamond!'

There was a gasp of admiration — followed by a dull thud. A curiously huddled figure lay in the middle of the floor. Robert had fainted!

6

Waiting

Half an hour had elapsed before he regained consciousness; a circumstance that caused Doctor Prescott no slight uneasiness.

Since Robert had retired to his room somewhere about an hour ago, he had been almost completely forgotten — except by one person in whose heart he occupied a much firmer place than he deserved. It was no wonder, therefore, that everybody was amazed to see him now stretched out and motionless upon the floor.

Doctor Prescott took charge of proceedings right from the beginning. In obedience to his orders, Robert was at once carried by Paul and Tony to the settee by the window, where he was then laid flat while the rest of the guests were sternly ordered to keep their distance to allow him the full benefit of the cool air from the open windows.

This new development left poor Thelma in an absolute haze. His quarrel with Paul — more than likely about her — she could understand; his strange manner at dinner; his drunkenness — yes, all these she could understand; she could even find it in her heart to make excuses for him, believing that they all sprung originally from the deep love he bore her. But why he should have crept into the room like a ghost, without anyone noticing him — and why he should collapse at the mention of a perfectly ordinary thing like a diamond ring — these things were too much for her!

She was the first to reach him after his fall, and stood anxiously by his side during the half-hour he remained unconscious. So near to him was she that she was the only person to overhear his first remark on coming to. This remark was a curious one, and contained only two words, 'diamond ring', which were repeated several times. The first time she heard it, Thelma found herself on the point of repeating it to those around her. But something seemed to prevent her. It was as though a voice had whispered into her ear the command of secrecy.

These words from Robert were followed by a slight twitching of the eyelids, and her heart seemed to flutter up into her throat as she saw the colour creeping back into his cheeks. His eyes slowly opened; a blank, uncomprehending stare filling their usually expressive depths. He looked around the throng of spectators, at the doctor, Paul, Isador — then his eye fell upon Thelma, when understanding returned in a flash, and he knew at once where he was.

Doctor Prescott stepped forward again. 'How are you feeling now, Mr. Harcourt?' he enquired.

Robert smiled weakly. 'Not so bad,' he said in a strange faraway voice. 'I . . . ' He paused. 'How did it happen?'

'You just fainted, that's all,' Paul said.

'Fainted? But why? What for?'

Once more, Thelma was on the verge of speaking when that strange force again exerted itself and froze the words before they passed her lips.

'It isn't the first time, you know,

Robert,' said Benjamin quietly.

'What do you mean, Mr. Fredericks?' the sick man asked weakly.

'Yes — what do you mean, Benjamin?' Even Doctor Prescott's curiosity had been aroused.

'Why, the same thing happened the last time he was here, or practically the same thing — about three or four days ago.'

'You never told me, Daddy.' Thelma's voice rang out with unexpected fervour.

'I didn't want to trouble you, dear. And anyway, he wasn't out for so long that time — only about ten minutes. It was after all the others had gone to bed. We were having a little talk in the study. You remember, Robert?'

'Yes, I remember.' His voice still sounded strangely distant, and his eyes fixed themselves upon the diamond ring Benjamin was now wearing with the most uncanny, fascinated stare.

'Something wrong about that. Young man like you, fainting twice in a week,' the doctor muttered gruffly. 'You must come and see me; let me overhaul you.'

'I will.'

'Sure you're all right now, Robert?' Thelma asked.

'Quite sure, thank you.' The queer singsong inflection he gave to the words did nothing to add to their conviction.

'I suggest you go straight off to bed,' the doctor advised him. 'A good night's rest'll do you the world of good.'

Robert sat bolt upright. 'No — no, I can't go to bed, yet. I — I couldn't sleep.'

'Of course you could. Come on! I'll give you a sleeping draught, if you think you'll need one.' With an indulgent smile, the old doctor leant forward to assist him to his feet. But this proved unnecessary; he was up in an instant.

'No — it's not that,' he cried, fencing desperately. 'It's just that I can't go to bed yet. Not just yet. Soon I will, I promise you. I'll go for a stroll. Just a stroll — in the garden.' He jumped to his feet and threw open the windows. 'I shan't be long — then I'll go straight to bed. Just a little air — only a little. Then to bed — straight to bed.' And without waiting for further argument, he stepped out into the blackness and disappeared from sight.

The doctor gave a grunt of annoyance. Thelma touched him lightly on the arm. 'Let him go, Doctor,' she said, with a wan smile. 'He knows best.'

'With all due respect to you, darling, I think he's a madman,' declared Paul with his usual smirk.

Benjamin and Isador nodded their heads in puzzled agreement as they all slowly drifted back to the fireplace, where Virginia and Tony were already standing, seemingly involved in a deep conversation all of their own. As it happened, they were the only ones out of the whole party who failed to express any sort of opinion on Robert's behaviour. They seemed to have almost succeeded in overlooking it entirely, so wrapped up were they in their own affairs, whatever they might be.

The clock on the mantelpiece struck a quarter to eleven. 'Nearly eleven already?' Isador said. 'I must be going.'

'You live on the other side of the wood, don't you, Mr. Fredericks?' the doctor enquired casually.

'Yes; it's not far really. Just follow the road that skirts the wood, that's all. It's called Glencroft. Not another house as far as you can see.'

'Don't you get lonely, Uncle?' Virginia asked, having broken off her conversation with Tony directly Isador started to speak.

'I like it, my dear. You must come over and see it, if you're interested.'

'I'd love to.'

'Well, now I really must be going.' Isador began to shake hands all round.

'Don't ring for Parker, dear. I'll see him out myself,' Benjamin cautioned as Virginia was about to press the bell.

'Good night, Uncle. And now there's no excuse for not coming to see us again.'

'Never fear, I shall come.'

She smiled affectionately as Benjamin took his brother by the arm and together they walked into the hall. For some few seconds they were silent. Then, just as they were within sight of the front door, Benjamin spoke. 'Well? Glad you came?'

'More than glad.'

'Good. What do you think of the children?'

'Charming. Virginia especially. The other one's your favourite, though, isn't she?'

'Thelma? I suppose she is. Do you think it's wrong to have favourites?'

'Not wrong. One can't help it.'

'I'm glad you understand.'

By this time Benjamin had helped his brother into his overcoat, and they were standing by the front door; Isador, hat in hand, slowly pulling on one of his gloves.

'You loved her mother, too, didn't you?' Isador said.

The question sounded rather harsh, and Benjamin resented it. 'You know I did. I told you so before.'

'That's why I've renewed our friendship. It's made me sympathise with you. Made you a better man, too.'

'It's made *me* sympathise with *you*.'

Isador shook his head contemptuously. 'It's too late for that, Benjamin. There's only one person I can accept sympathy from now, and that's — '

'Virginia? Well, I hope you'll become good friends.'

'Yes. How like her mother she is.'

'Isn't she?' Benjamin's voice was low and vibrated strangely with the emotion he was feeling.

'That's why I want you to be friends. It's the only reparation I can make you.'

Isador turned hurriedly away and opened the door. 'It seemed almost like the hand of fate that we should meet again after all these years,' he said with a complete change of tone. 'Almost as though it were intended.'

'Perhaps it was. It was certainly a coincidence.'

'My house — miles from anywhere. And you, and your car that had a breakdown on the way home. It's strange. A chance in a million. Why should your car have broken down outside my door? Why not someone else's? Why, out of all the millions of houses, should it have been outside mine?'

'Come to that, why should Helen have chosen this part of the country to make our home in? It was purely intuition on her part. She'd never been here before. She just fell in love with this particular plot of land the moment she set eyes on it.'

'There you are then.' Isador put his hat on, adjusting it slowly to his liking.

'Fated, Benjamin. It's a pity you're not more interested in psychic matters, for you might feel the significance of it.'

'But I *am* interested in them — up to a point.'

'That's no use. You must make a study of them — make them a life's work, an obsession if you like. Then you'll get somewhere, and begin to understand.' He broke off and looked at Benjamin strangely. '*I*'ve made a study of them,' he declared impressively. 'I know things — I have intuitions. Why, I could tell you something at this moment about yourself that would . . . But no, you'd only laugh.'

'Of course I wouldn't. Try me and see.'

'Waste of time. Besides, I've no facts to support it. So we'll say no more about it.' Thus dismissing the subject, he turned and faced his brother, holding out his hand. 'Good night, Benjamin,' he said. 'Don't trouble to come down to the car with me; I can look after that myself. You get back to your guests.' They shook hands.

'You must come again.' Benjamin smiled. 'Whenever you like.'

'I will. Sooner than you expect. Good

night!' And turning his back, he was swallowed up in the darkness.

Benjamin closed the door behind him. As he walked back towards the lounge, he passed Virginia and Tony, who were standing at the bottom of the stairs.

'I'm just going up to bed, Father,' she said.

He looked at his watch. 'At five past eleven? That's not like you, is it?'

'No, it isn't. But I'm still pretty tired, you know. In fact, I think it'll take a good night's rest to put me right again.' She drew her arm across her forehead. 'I've had some trouble with the car tonight, too,' she added.

'Oh? What was the matter?' Benjamin enquired, trying for once to show an interest in his daughter's conversation.

'Nothing much, I don't think. Carburettor blocked, possibly. Something quite simple. Only, I didn't feel well enough to do anything about it at the time.'

'I'll tell Jones to do it for you.'

'Oh no you won't,' Virginia retorted, holding up her hand imperiously. 'Nobody touches that car but me. I'm a jolly good mechanic. I shall be all right in the morning; I can see to it then.'

'Just as you like. But you won't be able to use Thelma's unless you ask her for it. She locks it now, you know.'

'I know she does, but I'll manage; thanks all the same.'

'Not at all.' And with a formal smile of courtesy, he turned and proceeded on his way.

'Good night,' Virginia called out after him.

'So you had trouble with the car, did you? Was that what kept you so long?' Tony's voice sounded different; quite brisk and incisive.

Virginia turned to him, an unhappy expression clouding her countenance. 'Partly,' she admitted. 'I can't tell you here, Tony. You must see that.'

'When *will* you tell me, then?'

'I don't know,' she said at length. 'Perhaps I shall never tell you.'

'Why not?' Tony positively snapped it out. If Thelma could have seen him now, how different her opinion would have been!

'It's something private, Tony. I — I wasn't expecting it. You must give me time to think it over. I may not be able to tell anybody.'

'Not even me?' He had changed his crisp delivery now for one of soft persuasion. As Virginia looked at him, her eyes began to glisten as though with tears she could hold back no longer. 'Do you believe I love you? Do you trust me?'

'You know I do,' she said.

'Have I ever let you down?'

'Of course you haven't. But — '

'Then why are you letting me down now, by keeping this secret from me? If it's about what I think it is, it's far too serious.'

'Do you think I don't realise that?'

'I know you do, dear. But we're in on this together, aren't we? It's too big a job for either of us alone. We must have no secrets from each other.'

She cast a nervous glance towards the open door of the lounge, whence the sound of voices could be heard from time to time in desultory conversation. Then she caught hold of his sleeve with fingers that he felt, to his surprise, were trembling.

'Tony,' she whispered, 'will you let me make one request before I tell you?'

'Go ahead.'

'Will you — will you meet me down here after they've all gone to bed tonight?'

'But why not tell me now?' he asked.

'That's impossible. We might be overheard. And that would be — fatal!'

'I haven't the slightest idea what it's all about,' he said, completely baffled, 'but I suppose I'll have to agree.'

'Bless you.' She bent forward and kissed him gently on the lips.

He smiled back at her. That kiss had worked wonders. He would ask no more questions now, and would have gladly followed her through hell had she so desired it.

'About twelve o'clock? In the lounge? That do?'

'Right.'

'Good night, darling.' She kissed him again and turned to go. 'I'm more grateful to you than you'll ever know.' She ran up the stairs and disappeared from his sight.

He walked thoughtfully back to the lounge.

'Hello, Tony!' Paul said. 'Thought you'd gone to bed.'

'No; I was just talking to Virginia,' he replied with a return to his assumed air of boredom.

'Bed?' Doctor Prescott muttered, drowsily echoing Paul. 'I think that's a jolly good idea.'

'So do I,' Paul joined in rather unexpectedly.

The doctor crossed to Benjamin and Thelma, who were standing by the fireplace, and shook hands with them. 'Good night, both of you,' he said.

Paul came across the room and did likewise, except he, deeming it his right as her future husband, subjected Thelma to a long embrace, to which she tried her utmost to respond; unfortunately, for both of them, without success.

'What say we all go to bed?' he said, addressing himself to Benjamin, after he had released her.

'I want to have a little talk with Thelma first. You go along. We'll follow you.'

'Right.' He turned to Tony. 'You coming too?'

'Yes, I think so,' he replied, stifling a yawn.

After his display of energy in the hall a few moments ago, this seemed somewhat strange. It was lucky for him that none of these people had been present at that little scene, or he might have had some awkward queries to answer. With a sleepy good-night to the two by the fire, he and Paul went out, preceded by the doctor.

It was not until the door had closed behind them that Benjamin spoke again. 'Sit down, my dear,' he said, motioning Thelma to an armchair.

She obeyed, her eyes fixed upon him in mute patience, waiting to hear what he had to say.

'Thelma, dear.' His voice was soft and tender. 'I want to ask you something — something that may hurt you very much. But I hope you'll answer.'

'Of course, Daddy.'

'Are you — still in love with Robert, my dear?'

A hurt expression like that of a

wounded animal leapt into her eyes. 'I *do* love him, Father. I can't deny it, even to myself. I've tried to, God knows. I don't want to love him — I don't want to! It's not a pleasant thing — it's hateful! But I can't kill it. I've tried, and I can't!' She buried her face in her hands in an agony of despair.

'My poor darling.' Benjamin leant forward and stroked her hair gently, as though she were a little child again. 'I knew it. I only wanted to hear it from your own lips.'

'But what can I do?' she cried without raising her face. 'What can I do?'

'Marry Paul?'

The words were soft and unforced, like the rest of his conversation, but the effect they produced upon Thelma was to send a cold shiver down her spine. She remained silent.

'Now I know why you're marrying him,' Benjamin said at last, determined to help her fight this problem that he could see was causing her such dreadful anguish. 'To forget. That's why you're doing it, isn't it? Isn't it, dear?'

114

'That — and to please you, Father,' she replied at last. 'You like him, don't you?'

'Yes. Very much. But — '

'And you don't like Robert. You never did, you know.'

'I'm afraid not, Thelma.' This was said with reluctance, like one admitting defeat.

'Then that's why I'm marrying Paul. I want to please you — to make you happy. You see, you're the only person I've ever loved besides Robert.' She looked him straight in the eyes and spoke quietly and sincerely, without any trace of sentimentality.

'Did you love me more than — your mother then?'

'Much more.'

'My dear.' That was all he could trust himself to say. His voice was already well-nigh cracking with emotion, and it was some little time before he could control himself sufficiently to go on. 'You know you mean more to me than anything in this world, don't you?' he asked her rather unsteadily.

'Yes, Father, I know.'

'So you mustn't be afraid to consult me

before doing anything rash.'

'Like marrying Paul?'

'Well — er, yes. Think it over first. And whatever you do, don't on any account ruin your life just to please me.' He rose slowly to his feet. 'We'll discuss it again in the morning, shall we?'

'Just as you say, Father.'

'Very well. After breakfast, then.'

With a sudden smile, Thelma jumped up and threw her arms around his neck. 'You darling!' she cried, impulsively kissing him.

He held her tightly. Then all of a sudden let her go. 'Robert!'

He was looking over her shoulder towards the window. She followed his gaze. And in spite of every effort she exerted to control herself, she could not hold back the gasp of surprise that escaped her as her eyes fell upon the wild figure standing before them.

'I'd forgotten all about you,' said Benjamin, endeavouring to make his voice sound as normal as possible, while at the same time drawing Thelma closer to him.

'You're off to bed, I suppose?' Robert asked the question, but in tones so harsh and strained as to be hardly recognisable.

'Yes — er — we're the last to go, as a matter of fact,' Benjamin replied.

'Do you mind if I stay down here for a little while longer?'

'Of course not. Providing you turn the lights out after yourself. I expect the servants have gone to bed.'

'I'll see to that. Good night.'

'Good night.' And taking his daughter gently by the arm, Benjamin led her from the room.

Later, when the clock on the mantelpiece struck the half-hour, Robert lurched like a drunken man across to the door, shut it, and then switched out the lights. Feeling his way by chairs and tables, he reached an armchair facing the fire; with a grunt he sunk heavily into it.

All was silent, save for the ticking of the clock and an occasional crackle from the logs in the fireplace. The room was pitch-dark. Only faintly visible was the silhouette of a man sitting rigidly forward in his chair, his eyes — like burning coals

— fixed unwaveringly upon the hands of the clock, as they slowly crept towards the fatal hour of midnight!

7

The Clock Strikes . . . Midnight!

Eleven forty-five! The last chime faded away into the deathlike silence. Still the upright figure in the chair remained rigid, motionless; the eyes staring unblinkingly at the clock.

There was a slight creaking noise — a pause — then it was repeated. Robert did not hear it. It came again, louder, more confidently, as of somebody opening a door or window.

A gust of cold wind swept through the room. The curtains flapped silently to and fro. The window into the garden stood open for an instant, while a dark shape as of a man slipped into the room. Softly it was pulled to while the shape crouched back among the shadows.

The clock ticked away in the darkness; a second pair of eyes wandered restlessly round the room. For a few minutes not a sound broke the stillness.

There came a rustle, the creaking of a board, the tap of a hand as it felt its way along the wall, and the shape moved stealthily forward. It reached the door; slowly, almost imperceptibly, white nervous fingers sought the handle. Gradually, with infinite care, they began to turn it. The door was open; the handle was released. The shape melted back among the shadows, the sound of breathing barely audible from out of the gloom.

Still the ticking persisted! The man in the chair remained motionless as before.

Inch by inch the door was opened, until it was wide enough to permit the shape to pass through the aperture. With catlike stealth it slipped out into the hall, and the door was slowly closed behind it. A slight click denoted that the catch had slipped home. Again Robert was alone.

Outside, a strong wind began to get up. Clouds, black and ominous, scudded across the skies. Trees swayed their branches in rhythmic motion while their leaves quivered as though in fear of some oncoming storm. The air was charged with ominous suspense, and a sense of waiting took possession of the earth.

Not by the flicker of an eyelash did Robert move from his position. He was inanimate, cast in stone — a figure tensed and waiting for the moment when he should spring to life and go about his horrible task.

It still lacked five minutes to midnight. How slowly they seemed to pass . . . seconds slowly dwindling away. A deep unreasoning fear burnt inside him — held him back until the appointed time with bands of steel so strong that even he, in all his frenzy of desire, could not break them. What he would do when the time arrived, he scarcely knew. He hardly gave it a thought, being merely an instrument awaiting his instructions.

The minute hand quivered on the hour . . . An interminable, soul-racking pause when breathing, heart and pulse seemed to be suspended in eternity. Then — the clock boomed out its long-awaited message. Twelve times the bell tolled its sonorous note, and it was midnight. The hour had arrived!

A sigh of relief floated out upon the night air as Robert rose to his feet. It was the only outward manifestation he made. His eyes were still wide and staring, like those of someone in a trance, and his hands were held close to his sides, with fists clenched tightly. This time it needed no chairs to guide him towards his destination, no familiar objects to finger, or tables to support himself by, for he walked as in the full glare of day; steadily, confidently, and with uncanny noiselessness. The door swung open silently at his touch and closed as swiftly and soundless behind him. The hall stretched out before him in the blackness — a huge chasm, unpierced by any ray of light.

Yet not one mark of hesitation did he show, but stealthily proceeded to the foot of the staircase. A board creaked as he put his weight upon it. He stopped and waited patiently for the echo of it to die away before proceeding.

He reached the first landing; stopped a second and listened. At first the silence was unbroken. Then he heard them again — voices. Where they were coming from, he couldn't tell. One was a man's, and it was raised in anger. The other . . . he was not sure whether it belonged to a man or a woman. Then quite abruptly they ceased, and all was quiet once more.

Squaring his shoulders, Robert, with catlike stealth, turned down the passage with increasing speed. Suddenly, as though he had run up against an iron bar, he stopped, turning to face a door beside him. His eyes gleamed in the darkness as though to say, 'My task is nearly done.' He was standing outside Benjamin Fredericks' bedroom!

At his deft touch the door slid open; and thus he gained admittance to the chamber of his unsuspecting victim. He closed the door behind him and remained standing in the shadows without betraying his presence, hardly drawing a breath. The room was in darkness; it was some time before his eyes became accustomed to it. A thin streak of moonlight shone in through the slightly parted curtains, while at the far end he could at last dimly distinguish the outline of a large canopied bedstead.

The curtains quivered slightly as with a gust of wind; Robert's menacing figure glided swiftly across the room. He looked down at the bed. The bedclothes clearly showed him the form of a man — he was right! Instinctively he felt that the man sleeping so peacefully before him was Benjamin, his victim — he whom he had come to murder!

Slowly he raised his arms; his hands like talons, with fingers crooked, stretched out through the blackness. A hideous figure hunched itself over the bed, preparing to descend upon the sleeping man, when a beam of light cut across the length of the room — and a voice, so horror-stricken as to be scarcely audible, brought him, trembling in every limb, round to the window, the glare full on his terror-stricken face.

'Stop!'

The word, although authoritative in itself, was almost more like an entreaty than a command, such agony being expressed in the voice that pronounced it. The curtains were thrown back, and a figure holding a torch advanced into the room. Nearer it came, the blinding light still relentlessly focused on Robert's pallid features, until a form began to slowly take shape before his eyes. A soft, warm hand stretched out and took hold of his, while he felt himself being slowly led from the room.

The next thing he knew, he was out in the passage. The torch had been extinguished, but the soft little hand grasped his firmly still. He was at the end of the passage. They moved towards the window seat, as by common consent, and his hand was released. They sat. And it was then, in a fitful gleam of moonlight, that he first glimpsed his companion's face. He gave a gasp of dismay. Oh God! Why, of all people in the world . . . ? The pale, drawn features that confronted him were those of none other than Thelma!

They sat gazing at one another in an awed silence, each with eyes riveted upon the other's countenance in speechless curiosity. At last Robert could bear it no longer, and buried his face in his hands with a heartrending groan. 'How can I explain? How can I ever explain?' This cry of mute agony was wrung from his soul; it tore him, lacerated him with its dreadful intensity.

'Is there anything — to explain?' Thelma spoke haltingly, her voice sounding harsh and vibrant in its unwonted hardness.

Robert looked up into her accusing eyes. 'Yes — oh yes,' he murmured desperately. 'Please let me think. You don't know what I've been through.'

He felt exhausted; he was damp with cold sweat all over, and his legs and hands were still shaking violently. It was a terrible shock she had given him, similar to startling a person when they're in the midst of sleepwalking; a sudden return to life that jars the nerves and leaves one limp and weak as a child, freshly awakened from some hideous nightmare.

'What were you doing in my father's room? Explain that if you can!'

This time her words were a command, and in spite of his agitation Robert felt bound to obey them. 'I must have been — hypnotised,' he declared, as though the fact were just as incredible to him as to her.

And then, ignoring the scornful smile that quivered at the corners of her lips, he plunged in and told her, in a wild torrent of burning words, all that had led up to his entrance into her father's bedroom.

She listened, without ever interrupting him. But the smile had faded from her lips after the first few words, and a look of sympathy took the place of the horror-stricken gaze that had filled her eyes.

'And that's the truth, I swear it,' he concluded. 'You can tell me I was mad — I must have been. That I'm a potential murderer. Anything you like. But I'm not lying. It is the truth, every word of it. I was hypnotised — it was all forced upon me. I don't pretend to understand it. It's as fantastic to me as it is to you, but it's the only possible explanation. I haven't been normal throughout the whole evening, until now.' And again his head fell between his hands in speechless anguish.

Thelma stretched out her hand, but something seemed to hold her back, and instead of touching him she moved further away and sat looking at him pathetically. Inside she felt so desperately sorry for him; and yet — he had tried to murder her step-father! That was a fact that not all the pity in the world could wash away. If she had not stopped him at that moment, who knew what might have happened. In all probability, she would now be facing a murderer — and, worst of all, the murderer of the man she loved and respected.

As she looked at his bowed head and dejected form, she knew, although she was sincerely and deeply sorry, that she could never feel quite the same towards him ever again. For there was a stone wall between them now that had never been there before. Nothing he did now could make it possible for her to get beyond it.

'What's that?' Robert's hoarse whisper sounded tense, almost to breaking point.

She listened; not a sound disturbed the stillness. 'Nothing,' she assured him.

With a hasty glance about them, he once more transferred his gaze to the floor and sat staring grimly before him. His nerves were thoroughly on edge. Seeing this, Thelma refrained from pursuing the discussion, and for some time a deep silence fell between them. They just sat there staring before them, each busy with their own thoughts; neither moving nor looking at each other, but just sitting as though turned to stone. Why they stayed thus, neither of them knew. It was by unspoken consent.

At length the silence was broken once again by Robert. This time his voice was a little steadier, and the question he put more definite: 'What were *you* doing in Mr. Fredericks' room tonight? You came from behind the curtains, didn't you?'

'Yes. Father asked me to come and talk to him.' There was a curious strained quality about her voice. 'He came to my room and asked me to come along to his as soon as I'd changed.'

'Was it about something important?'

'I thought so — then!' This last remark was made defiantly; a new note had subtly entered into the conversation.

'Is it indiscreet to ask what — '

'Yes!'

'I'm sorry.' By some curious means, the tables seemed to have been reversed, for

Robert was now quite self-possessed, while Thelma sounded as though she were hovering on the verge of panic. 'Listen! D'you hear?'

'Yes. A creaking noise.'

'The stairs!'

'There it is again! Somebody's coming down!' Drawing her dressing-gown tightly around her, she shrank nearer to the man at her side. Something like pride thrilled through him as he felt her heart beating against his chest. Not for many months had they been so close.

'Can you hear anything now?' he asked.

'No.'

The noise had stopped. Thelma's grip on Robert's arm had begun to relax, when at the foot of the stairs leading to the next storey, dimly illuminated by the moonlight, there appeared — a figure!

The grip on Robert's arm was immediately tightened again. He watched in an awed silence as the figure slowly advanced down the hall towards them. It was somebody fully dressed, but — yes, wearing bedroom slippers. That much he could distinguish, but no more. The face was just a blur; and even the hands, which he afterwards discovered were firmly gripped by the sides, were quite indistinguishable in the dim light that stole in through the window behind them.

Nearer and nearer it came, until without the slightest warning, it stopped. Robert gave a gasp of surprise as he realised that for the third time that night, somebody was about to force an entrance into Benjamin Fredericks' bedroom.

'Virginia!' The cry rang out from his side. He turned to Thelma in amazement.

'But how — ?' he said.

The figure had turned and was now peering in their direction, obviously making an attempt to discover whence the interruption came.

Before Robert could do anything to prevent her, Thelma had run forward. 'Virginia! What on earth — ?' The sentence faded away in inarticulate noises as she reached the figure and a hand was clapped firmly over her mouth.

Robert rose to his feet in an effort to make out the features of this strange intruder through the darkness. But he could have spared his pains, for Thelma was slowly drawing the figure towards the window; and in a few seconds he saw, quite unmistakably, that she had been quite right, and it was Virginia who had so unexpectedly interrupted them after all.

They all three faced each other in the dim light, questions burning upon their lips. Then Thelma once again asked what she had tried to say before being so unceremoniously interrupted: 'Virginia! What on earth are you doing here?'

Her half-sister turned a slightly disdainful countenance upon her. 'Come to that, what are *you* doing here? Or Robert?' she demanded aggressively.

The question was quite in order, but for some reason Thelma hesitated to answer it. 'I — I came to see Father,' she managed to stammer out at last.

'At this time of night?'

'He came along to my room while I was changing. We'd been having a discussion downstairs, and he wanted me to come to his room in order to continue it.'

'Really?' Virginia's tone, as well as her

set expression, had become slightly con-temptuous; a fact Thelma noticed, not without a feeling of considerable irrita-tion.

'Don't you believe me?' she demanded brusquely.

'Of course I do. Tell me, what was the interesting discussion Father was so anxious to continue?'

'Nothing that I care to repeat,' she answered defiantly.

'Oh, I see!'

Robert stepped forward angrily. 'Why are you being so superior about everything?' he demanded. 'You know Thelma's speak-ing the truth.'

Virginia turned her supercilious gaze upon him, intent on holding her own with both of them. 'You must admit it's a bit fantastic. Secret discussions and clandes-tine meetings with her step-father in the middle of the night.'

'She's told you the truth!'

Virginia turned her back on him to continue the conversation in low tones with Thelma. 'Why all the mystery? If you had something to discuss, why didn't you do it in the lounge and be done with it?'

'Because we'd decided to talk it over in the morning after a good night's sleep.'

'If you were going to talk about it in the morning, then why are you so secretive now?'

'I've already told you, I will not discuss it with you!'

'Then perhaps you'll tell me, if you've had your talk with him, whether he's gone to bed or not?' she asked sarcastically.

'He's in bed and asleep — that's why I didn't disturb him.'

On hearing this, Virginia displayed, for the first time, an unaffected interest. She raised her eyebrows in surprise. 'After asking you to come and talk to him?'

'Yes.' Thelma bowed her head to avoid the other woman's piercing gaze.

'And where, may I ask, did you meet Robert?'

'I — I — ' She suddenly raised her eyes and faced Virginia defiantly. 'I refuse to answer any more of your questions,' she burst out hotly. 'Who are you to question me, anyway? This isn't an inquisition, is it?'

'Of course not, dear.' Robert strived to calm her down, but her fighting blood had been thoroughly roused. It wasn't at all like Thelma to behave in this manner; in fact at this particular moment she was greatly surprised at it herself. But Virginia's attitude was really too insufferable to be endured.

'What are *you* doing here?' The question was blunt and to the point; so was the answer.

'I came to see Father too.'

Robert could hardly believe his ears. 'To see Mr. Fredericks?'

'Precisely. Is that, by any chance, why you came?'

'Yes — er — I — '

'Father seems to have had quite a number of visitors tonight, doesn't he?' Virginia turned a beaming smile upon Thelma, who, flushed with annoyance, could think of no adequate retort, much as she desired to.

'Look!' It was Robert who spoke, pointing down the hall. Both women followed the direction of his finger. The door facing Benjamin's was slowly opening! 'Who sleeps

135

in that room?' he whispered tensely.

'I think — Tony does.' The name sprang to Thelma's lips as the form of a man crept out into the hall, carefully closing the door behind him.

Virginia caught them both by the arm. 'Don't make a sound!' she cautioned.

They watched, straining their eyes in their excitement, as Tony, without pausing or looking to right or left, made straight for the main staircase and disappeared into the blackness below.

'He's gone downstairs,' Robert said in surprise.

'Yes; he's gone to meet me. I promised to meet him in the lounge at midnight,' Virginia explained casually.

'But whatever for?' Thelma asked.

'That's an explanation that will keep,' was her step-sister's answer.

But will it? Thelma thought to herself; for instinctively she knew that once again in her questioning of Virginia, she was up against a brick wall. On the other hand, Virginia herself seemed to have dismissed it all completely from her mind.

At last Virginia turned to them with a

keen, eager look upon her face, and they knew whatever it was that had so enthralled her would soon be disclosed to them. As usual, she began with a characteristically strange remark: 'Father's not a very heavy sleeper, is he?' she asked quite suddenly. The question was addressed to Thelma, and all trace of standoffishness had vanished from her voice.

'No, he isn't,' she said. 'He's a light sleeper.'

Virginia nodded, having received the answer she expected. 'You knocked on the door before going in?' she continued.

'Why, yes.'

'And you, Robert?'

'I — I'm afraid I — '

'Whether you did or not, it doesn't matter; Thelma's should have been sufficient. You both went into the room, didn't you?'

'Yes.' Thelma answered for them both, while Robert just nodded, quite at a loss to understand what she was driving at.

'Curious. And he was expecting Thelma, too; that makes it doubly queer.'

'You're right,' said Robert, seeing the

trend of her thoughts at last. 'It's most odd!'

'What do you think, Thelma?'

'I — I don't know. I can't understand it.'

'Neither can I. Why don't we find out? Wake him up and see for ourselves.'

They all three moved up the passage towards Benjamin's room. This time they made no pretext of covering up their presence, but went boldly up to the door. Virginia knocked.

'Ssh! You'll wake the whole house,' Thelma whispered, a feeling of uneasiness creeping over her.

They waited, five, ten seconds. But not a sound stirred from within.

Robert's hand was already on the handle. 'We're going in,' he said quietly as he opened the door.

Inside, all was darkness as before. Even the moon seemed unable to penetrate this time, and the room stretched out before them like a vast cavern. Not a sound could be heard except that of the wind outside, which seemed to be growing stronger every moment. Carefully avoiding collisions with the furniture, they tiptoed in the direction of the bed, Robert leading. Stretching out his hand, he felt the bedclothes — and under them the figure of a man.

He shook it — at first gently, then a trifle more roughly. Still there was no response. There was a sudden click at his side, and a light came on. He looked quickly round. It was from a little reading lamp that stood at the side of the bed. Thelma took her hand away from the switch and tilted the shade so that all the light was focused on the bed.

Still the occupant of the bed made no movement. All they could see was a jumble of bedclothes. Robert leant over the pillow and drew them gently back.

A piercing scream from Thelma shattered the silence. A low cry broke from Virginia also, as Robert gave a gasp of horror.

For staring at them — ghastly in the glare from the lamp — were the hideously contorted features of Paul Conway!

8

Strangulation!

What happened immediately following this dreadful discovery, Robert never knew. He dimly remembered having covered up the dead man's face and taken each of the two terrified women firmly by the arm. The next thing he knew, they were outside in the passage.

'What's the matter? I thought I heard a scream,' a quiet, unobtrusive little voice asked near at hand. Turning, Robert saw Doctor Prescott hurrying down the passage towards them. He went forward to meet him, at the same time lowering his voice so as not to be overheard by the women.

'Something dreadful, Doctor,' he said. 'It's Paul. I think he's been murdered.'

'Murdered?' The doctor was wide awake upon the instant. 'Where is he?'

Robert pointed towards the room they

had just left. 'In there.'

Without another word, the little man hurried through the doorway and vanished from their sight. The three people left outside waited for his return in an agony of suspense. Robert felt, in some curious way, responsible for it all, remembering his own behaviour earlier in the evening.

His attention was soon drawn back to the door again, however, where he perceived the doctor looking in his direction. The expression on his face was sufficient to convey to Robert what he was about to say. 'I was right?' he asked in a tense voice.

'Quite right.'

Virginia looked towards the doctor. 'He was strangled, wasn't he?' she asked.

'Yes, my dear.'

'How horrible!' She bent down to comfort Thelma, who had begun to weep bitterly.

The doctor looked towards the women as though seeing them for the first time.

'They were with me when I — found him,' Robert explained, without waiting to be asked.

The doctor nodded. 'The question now is, what has become of Benjamin?'

'Mr. Fredericks?' Robert replied mechanically. 'But — ' Then it suddenly burst upon him. Good God! Benjamin Fredericks! Whatever could have happened to him? He looked at the women, who returned his gaze in blank amazement.

'Father!' The cry broke from Thelma as she buried her face against Virginia with a little sob.

'What can we do, Doctor?' Robert asked helplessly.

'Only one thing we can possibly do,' came the determined reply. 'Send for the police.'

'The police!' cried Robert, as both he and the women drew back in distaste.

The doctor looked at them rather quizzically. 'It's our duty. There's been a murder committed here, therefore the police should be informed at once.'

'But Mr. Fredericks?' Robert countered weakly.

'They will make it their business to find him too.'

Robert felt a sinking in the pit of his

stomach. The idea of the police, with their endless questions and examinations, sickened him. Besides, who knew what they might discover? What might not be brought to light in the event of an inquiry?

'What do you say, Robert?' The old man asked him this question in such a kindly tone that he felt deeply moved to agree with him. After all, they would have to be called in sooner or later; so, he asked himself, why not now and be done with it?

'You're right,' he admitted finally. 'I'll ring them.' He moved a few paces in the direction of the stairs, then turned. 'We'll all go down together, shall we?'

'A good idea,' replied the doctor as he stepped between the women and led them gently forward. And so they proceeded down the staircase into the darkened hall.

Robert switched on the light and crossed to the telephone, which stood in a little alcove near the lounge. Having lifted the receiver, he was just about to speak when the door leading to the lounge was thrown open — and Tony, still fully dressed, stood before them.

The remainder of Robert's conversation was completely lost amid the hubbub of explanations that ensued. At length he replaced the receiver and turned to them all. 'They'll be here in about fifteen minutes,' he announced loudly.

Everybody stopped talking, and they all slowly moved towards the lounge, there to await the police. The great room was bare and cold. Robert went immediately over to the fireplace and endeavoured to stir the dying embers into life. After a while he succeeded, while the others threw themselves into the easy chairs surrounding it. The strumming of fingers and tapping of feet, however, soon proclaimed the state of their nerves.

Robert rose to his feet and, finding a vacant chair just behind him, sank gratefully into it. It seemed strange that he of all people should have taken command of this crisis as he appeared to have done — but he was feeling a new man. Ever since he had caught that fleeting glimpse of Thelma's pale, drawn features in the moonlight by the window, he had found himself completely normal again. Perhaps it was the accusing look in her eyes that had wrought this change in him. Whatever it was, it had remade of him the man he had been before he let himself sink to his present level.

Encouraged by his reflections, he looked towards Thelma. But although he could not see her clearly, he felt again that coldness he had experienced earlier in the evening, and knew instinctively that it would take some tremendous action on his part to regain for him that place in her favour he had so wantonly thrown away. His gaze travelled to the doctor, who appeared lost in meditation; after which he sank back into a strange, tangled reverie of his own.

It was obvious that he had gone into that bedroom intending to commit a murder — and if it hadn't been for Thelma's timely intervention, he *would* have committed murder. Unless — and this was the one thought that cheered him — unless the murder had been committed before midnight. But if it had not been committed before midnight, who would take Thelma's word for it that she had stopped him in the eleventh hour before he had time to perform the crime he'd set his heart on? Nobody would believe it; that was apparent on the face of it. They'd say it was a story concocted by Thelma to save her ex-lover from the gallows.

And what had he to offer in his defence? A mad story of hypnotism, a fortune teller and a diamond ring. It was like a dream, a nightmare — the only difference being that he could remember it more clearly. How incredible it had seemed, even when he had been telling it to Thelma. And yet she had believed him, in spite of her antipathy at the start. Could it be that she still loved him?

Again he looked towards her. It couldn't be! That cold look; she couldn't love him any longer.

He gave a deep sigh. He felt himself in the hands of fate. What was to be, would be, and he could do nothing to alter it. It was the philosophy of despair he was repeating, but what else could he do?

The wind outside howled monotonously; the little group of people drew their chairs nearer to the fire. There was an icy blast that swept across the room like a tornado; the curtains billowed out as the window into the garden blew open noisily.

Robert rose and went to close it. As he did so, it started a train of thought. How long had it been open? Had it been open while he had been sitting in the darkness, waiting for the clock to strike midnight? Who was the last person to shut it? He tried to remember. Why, he was; he'd closed it after coming back from his ramble in the grounds when he had met Thelma and Benjamin going up to bed. But could he be certain he'd closed it properly? Considering the state of his mind at that particular moment, it was impossible to say what he had done or neglected to do. And that left the definite possibility of the window having been open ever since he went out into the garden, about two hours ago. Time enough for somebody to have slipped in unnoticed, even while he himself had been sitting in the room.

He knew nothing of Paul's private life; none of them did. He was definitely unpleasant, though, and it seemed more than likely that his aggressive manner must have earned him a great number of enemies. Supposing one of those enemies had followed him down to the manor house, waited for his opportunity, slipped in by the open window, murdered him, and then slipped out again and made his getaway? A credible theory, at all events, thought Robert as he fastened the catch. But how did this person get into the grounds in the first place? And how did he know the right bedroom to go to, even granting he succeeded in entering the house?

These questions puzzled him the more he thought of them. And in the midst of it all he came up against the question that overshadowed everything: namely, what was Paul Conway's body doing in Benjamin Fredericks' bedroom?

Everybody seemed to have acted so mysteriously. Virginia, for instance: why had she suddenly conceived the idea of visiting her father in the early hours? They weren't friendly, but on the contrary appeared not to have the slightest interest in common. If only she'd given some reason for it! But perhaps she was reserving that for the police.

And even Thelma, he had to admit, hadn't acted in such a straightforward manner as one might have expected from her. The story she had told of her father's request that she should come to his room seemed reasonable enough; but her refusal to divulge what the discussion was about rendered her position almost as unexplainable as her step-sister's.

And then last, but by no means least, there was the bored, seemingly completely disinterested Tony. What was he doing wandering down to the lounge at such an hour? Was Virginia's story to be believed? And if he had come down to meet her, what was it they had to discuss that could not have been broached earlier in the evening in the presence of the others? It was all rather overwhelming, and Robert felt himself sinking deeper into the morass at every step. Definitely a case for the police, he decided.

He looked round the room at his companions. The doctor was sitting back, lost in reflection. Virginia and Thelma, now quite recovered from her tears, were still carrying on a conversation in an undertone. And Tony had relaxed completely under the soothing influence of the now blazing fire, and was reclining in his chair with half-closed eyes, that lazy smile still playing about his lips, which had made him appear so conspicuously rude among the guests earlier in the evening.

Robert listened intently to try if he could hear an approaching car, but not a sound broke the stillness. Then came a deep rumble in the far distance. Thunder! At the same time he realised that the wind had suddenly whipped up. The storm was drawing nearer!

Almost at the same time that the distant clap of thunder proclaimed the arrival of the elemental storm, Thelma, unable to bear the tension any longer, burst out with a pathetic plea for action: 'Can't we do something? Must we sit here like dummies? Can't any of you do anything to help?'

'What can we do, Thelma?' Robert said.

'Find my father!'

'How can we do that? We shouldn't know where to begin. And we might spoil the ground for the police afterwards. We'd be hindering the search by trying to do anything by ourselves, not furthering it.'

'He's quite right, dear,' Virginia put in quietly.

'I don't believe it!' Thelma went on passionately, ignoring their efforts to calm her. 'There must be something we can do. Something we can — '

'There is,' the voice of the doctor boomed out with unexpected ardour. 'We can wake him up.'

'You know where he is?' Thelma asked unsteadily.

'Yes; that's what I've been trying to remember.'

'Where?'

'In the room occupied until tonight by the man we have just found — Mr. Paul Conway,' he announced. The others were staring at him in complete bewilderment. He leant forward and repeated in detail the scene of only a few hours previously, when Paul had complained to Benjamin concerning the discomfort of his bedroom. 'And so,' he said in conclusion, 'what I expected to happen has come to pass. Benjamin has given up his room to Paul, and if we go upstairs now I wager we'll find him safe and sound.'

Thelma gave a cry and jumped to her feet. 'We must go at once,' she shouted excitedly.

Robert rose to his feet also, prepared to lead the way. He walked briskly out of the room and across the hall in the direction of the staircase. Everybody followed at his heels. Still he was by some strange chance their leader, and nobody dreamed of questioning his right to be first in everything.

Up the stairs they marched in a purposeful line. As they disappeared round the bend in the staircase, Parker appeared from below. Evidently something of the noise they had been creating had reached the servants' quarters, for a small group of alarmed-looking women clustered around him nervously, asking him questions as to what it was all about. Parker, striving to look dignified in an old dressing-gown and with his sparse hair in wild disarray, replied to their queries in well-modulated tones, trying to give the impression that all was as it should be. In spite of this commendable restraint, however, the hubbub among his colleagues increased with amazing speed.

Upstairs, the party had reached the first landing and were just ascending the second flight of stairs, which led to the top floor, on which were situated the bedrooms until recently occupied by Virginia and Paul. Arriving at their objective, they turned sharply to the right and proceeded down the corridor, still in single file.

Robert passed Virginia's room and came to a halt before the door next to it. He raised his hand and banged loudly.

A loud crash boomed out near at hand, followed by an ominous rumble. The storm was nearly upon them; outside the rain began to fall.

But still no sound came from behind

the door. Robert raised his arm and banged again, even louder than before. Supposing the old man was there — might he not have been murdered also? A feeling of terror gripped at their heartstrings.

The rain came down in torrents, while the thunder, growing louder every minute, became more frequent.

It was in the midst of one of these bursts of thunder that the door was slowly opened to disclose to them the sleepy, tousled-headed figure of Benjamin Fredericks.

For a few seconds he stood staring at them in a dazed kind of wonderment. But before he found time to speak, Thelma had pushed her way forward and thrown herself into his arms. 'Oh, Father! Father!'

He looked down on her tenderly, but his expression of wonderment grew even more pronounced. 'What is the meaning of all this?' he asked.

Robert stepped forward, lowering his voice. 'It's Paul,' he said gravely. 'He's been murdered — in your room.'

'In my — ?'

But before the older man could finish what he had to say, there came another crash of thunder, so deafening as to render any further statement inaudible. As it died away this time, there came another sound to take its place: the loud clanging of a bell.

Robert stepped back with a sigh of relief. He raised his eyes and met the questioning look in Benjamin's without discomfort. For he was no longer a leader — his responsibility was over; and from now on he was one of them. The police had arrived!

9

The Inquiry Begins

Downstairs, everything was in an uproar, the arrival of the police throwing the already curious band of servants into a state of abject panic. All their worst suspicions seemed to be immediately confirmed — there had been a murder! It never occurred to them that the arrival of the police might be explained away by any other circumstance.

Who was the victim and who the criminal? Their choice of victim was Benjamin — merely because he had not made up one of the party they had just seen going upstairs. It was, therefore, a terrific shock to them all when Benjamin appeared in person at the head of the stairs, apparently quite unharmed and very much alive. He had hastily slipped on a dressing-gown, having been told of the arrival of the police by Robert, and was now fully prepared to face up to the whole unpleasant business.

The others followed close upon his heels and advanced quietly and deliberately down the stairs to meet the two plainclothes men, accompanied by a sergeant, who awaited them in the hall.

'Good evening, gentlemen! I understand you were telephoned for, without my knowledge, about twenty minutes ago?' Benjamin's voice, though subdued, was clear and self-possessed.

The larger of the two plainclothes men stepped forward. 'That's right, sir,' he said. 'Something about a murder. I'm Detective Blake.' He turned to the little white-haired man by his side. 'And this is Detective Inspector Coleman.'

'Your information is unfortunately correct,' Benjamin replied in the same steady, impersonal tone. 'There has been a murder committed here. One of my guests has been strangled. You will find him upstairs in my room. Doctor Prescott, another guest of mine, will furnish you with any further details you may require.'

At the conclusion of these words, the

man addressed as Detective Inspector Coleman suddenly became immensely active. His precise voice punched out his orders: 'Sergeant Ridgeway! You remain down here. Blake, come upstairs with me. Doctor Prescott?'

'Yes?' The doctor stepped forward and stood beside Benjamin.

'You can show us the way. Where does that door lead to?' He pointed to the one at the end of the hall.

Benjamin answered him: 'The lounge.'

'Good. You'd all better wait in there until we come down.'

'Very well.' Benjamin led the way into the lounge while the others followed him, the sergeant bringing up the rear.

Coleman turned to the servants clustered together in a terrified group — with the exception of Parker, who stood his ground valiantly. 'You all remain where you are until I return. Sergeant Ridgeway, leave the door to the lounge open and see nobody leaves the house.'

He turned away, and accompanied by Blake and the Doctor, mounted the stairs. But when they arrived at the top and the doctor had pointed out Benjamin's room to them, he found himself abruptly dismissed and given orders to join the others in the lounge.

The detectives stood looking gingerly round the room as Blake began to feel for the light switch. There was a slight sound as the light flashed on; a second's silence as they stood quite still; but the room was exactly as when the doctor had left it a few moments before.

Coleman crossed swiftly to the bed. The sight that greeted him was sufficiently horrible to make even his steely nerves flinch: a dreadful blackened face, a swollen protruding tongue, hideous glazed eyes, and a fixed expression of paralysed terror. He turned to Blake, who had come up behind him. 'Death by strangulation?'

Blake nodded.

'How long before the police-surgeon can get here?'

'About twenty minutes now, I should think.'

'Well, we can't do much until he arrives.' Coleman covered up the contorted face of the dead man and then turned back to his assistant with renewed energy. 'I'll go downstairs and try to get something out of those people,' he said, 'while you stay here and see what you can find; only be very careful not to touch anything.'

'Very good, sir.'

Near the foot of the stairs, he caught up with the doctor, who, lost in meditation, was still slowly wandering, with frequent halts, down towards the hall.

'Hi, Doctor! I want you.'

The little man jumped as though coming out of a deep reverie.

'Is there a study or something of the sort I can use around here?'

'Why, yes. There's Benjamin's study, of course. Mr. Fredericks'.'

By this time they had reached the hall, and Doctor Prescott turned in the direction of the lounge. 'Hadn't we better ask him first . . . ?'

'That's all right. Sergeant Ridgeway!'

From his position in the open doorway, the sergeant sprang rather heavily to attention.

'Tell Mr. Fredericks I'm using his study

for the moment, and I hope he won't mind.'

'Yes, sir.'

He turned on his heel and disappeared into the lounge. 'Show me,' the inspector commanded.

The doctor conducted him past a large bench, where the little band of servants had seated themselves, towards the front door. Just before reaching this, he stopped and pointed to a door on his left.

'Here?' the Inspector inquired, and without waiting for a reply he threw it open, switched on the light and marched into the room beyond.

There was revealed to him a beautifully oak-panelled apartment, complete with heavy, dark furniture, all of which was dominated by a massive writing-desk in the middle of the floor. This he made a line for at once. Seating himself in the high-backed chair behind it, he placed his notebook and fountain-pen before him, and fixed the doctor with his piercing grey eyes.

'Sit down, Doctor; I want to ask you one or two questions,' the Inspector said civilly enough.

The little man closed the door behind him and settled in a chair opposite the inquisitor.

The storm had passed over, and the two men faced one another in silence, only broken by the monotonous drip-dripping from beyond the window.

'First of all,' Coleman began, 'you must understand that everybody is necessarily under suspicion.'

'I noticed that,' the doctor replied ruefully, recalling to mind his unceremonious dismissal upstairs.

'Well, now that you understand, we can proceed. You're under no obligation to answer any of the questions I may put to you, but I trust you and your fellow guests will do everything in your power to help clear up this mystery that surrounds you all.'

'You may rely on my assistance wherever you think it necessary.'

'Thank you.' Coleman permitted himself a courteous smile, then he leant forward, the pen poised in his hand. 'Can you tell me who first discovered the body?'

'Mr. Harcourt. I met him outside with

the two young ladies.'

'In what position did you find the body?'

'Lying in the bed on the right side, and practically covered over with the blankets.'

'And did you question Mr. Harcourt and the ladies as to what they were doing up at that time of the night?'

'No. I was far too surprised to say anything. And Harcourt stepped forward immediately and informed me of the murder.'

'What did you do?'

'I went inside to see if what he had told me was correct — that Paul Conway was lying strangled in Mr. Fredericks' bedroom.'

'Which you subsequently found to be the case?'

'Yes.'

'And after this, Mr. Harcourt still made no effort to explain either his own or the ladies' presence at such a late hour?'

'No. He merely said they had been with him when he found the body. It was their screams that awakened me.'

'I see. And in the course of verifying his statement, did you have occasion to touch the body?'

'Naturally. I made a cursory examination of it.'

'And then?'

'I asked what had become of Mr. Fredericks. But none of them seemed to have given that a thought. So I suggested calling in the police.'

'How did they take that?'

'At first they seemed a little unwilling, but they soon gave way and Harcourt rang up the station.'

'And after that, what did you do?'

'Well, as far as I can remember, it was then we met Tony. The fair-haired young man; Tony Hargreaves.'

'Was he wandering about too?'

'I suppose so. He suddenly appeared from the lounge.'

'Hm. And did he offer you any explanation?'

'He was never asked for one. By that time we were all far too worried about Mr. Fredericks to think of anyone else.'

'I see. And how did you find Mr.

Fredericks in the end?'

'Well, I remembered something that had occurred earlier in the evening, and — '

The doctor gave an account of the scene between Benjamin and Paul in the lounge, and a still further resumé of events leading up to the discovery of Benjamin and the arrival of the police.

'Thank you, Doctor,' Coleman said when he had finished. 'A very full statement. All this, you say, happened shortly after midnight. And now, would you mind telling me what your exact position in this household is?'

'I'm one of Benjamin's oldest friends. Today's his birthday, and I came over to celebrate it.'

'I see. Quite a party, in fact. And the two young ladies? His daughters?'

'Virginia is the dark one; Thelma is his step-daughter. Her full name's Thelma Bancroft.'

'And this Mr. — ' He consulted his notes. ' — Hargreaves?'

'Virginia's fiancé.'

'May I take it then that Mr. Harcourt is

engaged to the younger one?'

'He was. She broke it off a few days ago.'

'And what position did Mr. Conway hold in the household?'

'He — he was Thelma's new fiancé,' the Doctor replied, a note of indecision creeping into his voice for the first time.

'Rather a sudden engagement, wasn't it? How long have they known each other?'

'About six weeks, I think.'

The inspector made a note of it.

Doctor Prescott shifted uneasily in his chair. 'I don't want you to think that — ' he blurted out awkwardly.

'Yes, Doctor?'

'Nothing.' He suddenly realised that his words might be misconstrued as evidence against Robert; but faced with the shrewd glance of the inspector, the words of defence died upon his lips. Had he known how much value those few words might have been towards establishing Robert's innocence, he would most certainly have plucked up sufficient courage to speak them.

'That will do for the present, Doctor. You may rejoin your friends in the lounge.'

'Thank you.' He rose wearily to his feet, suddenly realising how dreadfully tired he was. He left the room and returned to the lounge, where Sergeant Ridgeway stood aside for him to pass. No sooner was his entrance noted than he was surrounded, questions from the two women being shot at him with a rapidity which left no time for him to reply. The hubbub was curtailed almost at once by the sergeant, who announced in his loud stentorian tones that the inspector wished to see Mr. Fredericks in the study at once.

Without any visible signs of annoyance or perturbation, Benjamin answered the summons immediately. At his entrance, Coleman looked up and waved him peremptorily towards the chair facing him. As Benjamin seated himself, the inspector eyed him intently before speaking. 'Mr. Fredericks,' he said — and Benjamin was amazed at the sympathy with which he spoke, 'I fully realise what a dreadful affair this is for you; and you may be sure I shall spare you

167

all I possibly can . . . '

'Thank you, Inspector.'

' . . . but I'm afraid I'm bound to question you upon one or two points, although owing to the lateness of the hour I promise to confine myself to the merest essentials. First, I want you to give me a detailed account of your movements last night from, say, about half past eleven until you were awakened.'

'At half past eleven,' Benjamin answered promptly, 'Thelma and I had just left the lounge and were mounting the stairs on our way to bed. We were the last to go excepting Robert, who said he wished to stay up a little longer. I wished her good night on the landing and we both proceeded to our own rooms. I had barely finished changing, however, when it suddenly occurred to me how much fairer it would be to Thelma if we concluded the conversation we had been having downstairs tonight, instead of leaving it over until the morning as I had previously suggested. I carefully crept down the passage to her room and rapped on the door. After a few seconds she put her head round, and I asked her to come along to see me directly she'd changed, as I'd had a new idea I wished to discuss with her. She said she'd be along in a few minutes, and with that I returned to my own room.

'On opening the door, I found to my great surprise that Paul was sitting on the edge of the bed, presumably waiting for my return. He told me that all he had said concerning his room — which he'd complained to me about it earlier in the evening — had been perfectly justified and that he really couldn't stay there. He was suffering from neuralgia, he declared; and what with that and the noises from the pipes in the bathroom next door, he was finding it impossible to sleep. In short, he asked me point blank if I would exchange bedrooms with him.

'I was a little annoyed by this demand on his part, but as his host I had no choice but to accept. So up to the third floor I trudged; and I'm sorry to say, Inspector, that my irritation caused me to completely overlook my arrangement with Thelma — it wasn't a very important matter we had to discuss, anyway — and I went straight to bed. I fell asleep almost at once and knew nothing more until I heard Robert and the others banging upon the door to tell me of this terrible murder that had been committed under my roof.'

'I see. That accounts for you pretty thoroughly, doesn't it? What time was all this?'

'Roughly about ten to twelve.'

'And now I should like you to tell me all you can about the dead man. He was engaged to your step-daughter, wasn't he?'

'Only recently. As a matter of fact, Inspector, I haven't known him myself for longer than a few weeks. You see, he used to run a private detective agency, and I happened to meet him over some little trouble I had, and — '

'I take it you are now retired, Mr. Fredericks?'

'Well, yes; to all practical purposes, at any rate. But I occasionally revert to my old business and allow myself a little flutter on the stock exchange, just to amuse myself, you know; and it was in connection with one of these little flutters of mine that I first met Paul Conway.'

From this point onwards, he began to speak more quickly, as though from a desire to lay whatever information he might have speedily and unreservedly at the inspector's feet.

'I went to him with a good personal introduction,' he continued, 'and consequently came to know him better than I should have done otherwise. We soon became friends. He seemed a charming young man, and it wasn't long before he had taken me completely into his confidence. It appeared that the detective agency was merely a sort of game to him, for in reality he was the possessor of a large private income that made work of any sort quite unnecessary, except as a means of passing the time. Well, our friendship proceeded, and then one night I asked him down here to dinner. He came — saw Thelma, and instantly fell in love with her. Naturally I was delighted, as she seemed to reciprocate his feelings also, and made it my business to encourage them in every way possible

— with the result that this evening I had the great pleasure of announcing their engagement. And that, Inspector, is all I can tell you about Paul Conway.'

'Not quite all, I think. Why did you look upon this young man as so eligible a suitor for your step-daughter, Mr. Fredericks?' Coleman asked.

'But I've already told you that. He was well off, and — '

'Was it not because you thought he might help her to forget her former engagement?'

'Her engagement to Robert, you mean?'

'Yes. How long did that engagement last?'

'About three years, I think.'

'Three years?' The Inspector spoke sympathetically. 'Now come, Mr. Fredericks, I can understand your feelings; but you can't hurt anybody by speaking the truth, you know, unless it's the guilty person.'

Benjamin looked away, acutely embarrassed. 'To tell you the truth, Inspector,' he replied at last, with regret, 'it was because of Robert that I did it. But he's not a bad chap, really he isn't — he's a little weak, that's all!'

'Drink?'

'Just a bit. Lately he's let himself go to pieces. Only tonight he collapsed in the lounge; and he did the same thing the last time he was here. Doctor Prescott says it's burning the candle at both ends, but what with that and his uncontrollable temper, he's obviously no fit match for Thelma.'

'Have you — er, seen him in one of these tempers recently?'

'Tonight.'

'With whom?'

'Paul Conway,' Benjamin murmured, scarcely above a whisper.

'The murdered man,' Coleman exclaimed sharply. 'D'you know what it was about?'

'They wouldn't tell us. We came in at the end. Just in time to — separate them. Robert had Paul by the throat. Thelma called out, and he let him go.'

The inspector gave a deep sigh of satisfaction. At last he felt he was getting somewhere. 'One more question, Mr. Fredericks,' he said, his eyes even brighter than usual, searching Benjamin's face intently. 'This conversation of yours with your step-daughter — might I suggest that it concerned Robert Harcourt?'

'You may suggest anything you like, Inspector, but that is a point on which I should prefer to give no answer.'

'Very well. But you can surely tell me why he and Miss Fredericks should wish to enter your room at so late an hour?'

'No, I cannot. I'm just as much in the dark about that as you are, Inspector.'

Coleman leant back and his face expanded into a smile. 'Thank you, Mr. Fredericks,' he said. 'You've been very helpful. You will oblige me now by returning to the lounge and remaining there for the present. I promise to let you all get to your beds at the first possible opportunity.'

'Thank you, Inspector.' Benjamin rose unsteadily to his feet and walked towards the door. He had suddenly gone very pale, and halfway across the room he put his hand out to steady himself.

Coleman jumped up instantly and came to his assistance. 'Feeling ill? Perhaps you'd better go straight to bed.'

174

'No, I'm all right,' came the weak reply. 'Nothing serious . . . I'm all right, really I am.'

By this time they had reached the door, and Coleman opened it. 'Sergeant Ridgeway!' he called. Ridgeway ran laboriously across the hall. 'Help Mr. Fredericks back to the lounge. He's not feeling too well.'

'Yes, sir.'

He stood watching for a few seconds as the sergeant assisted Benjamin clumsily across the hall and into the lounge beyond.

'He is a sick man, too,' he said as though in answer to his own thoughts, returning to his seat behind the desk, 'I shouldn't give him long for this life. Don't like that colour of his.'

He looked down at the notes he had written, and the smile returned once more to his face. Things seemed to be taking shape already. Why, this looked like being the easiest case he'd ever had the luck to tackle. Good thing for him, too, if he managed to solve it straight away; possibly promotion.

His pleasant reverie was disturbed by the clanging of the bell. A few seconds later, there came a discreet rap on the door. 'Come in!'

Sergeant Ridgeway came a little way into the room. 'The police surgeon, sir.'

'Oh yes, take him upstairs. And send Miss Bancroft in to me. She's the fair young lady.'

The sergeant withdrew, and Coleman returned to the perusal of his notes; until he was disturbed by another rap on the door.

'Come in!'

This time it was Thelma, and she advanced into the room, an angry flush staining her cheeks.

'Inspector,' she said in a grieved tone, clasping her dressing-gown tightly around her, 'I've just asked the sergeant to allow me to go upstairs to change, but . . . '

Coleman rose to his feet, interrupting her with that charming smile which he seemed able to assume at will.

'If it were necessary I should be only too delighted for you to change, Miss Bancroft,' he declared suavely, 'but I'm hoping that I shall soon be able to allow you all to return to your beds.'

'But Father, can't he — ?'

'I have already told your father that he is at liberty to go to bed whenever he wishes.'

'Oh — thank you.'

'Not at all. Now, won't you be seated.'

He motioned her to the chair facing him; she meekly obeyed, now lulled completely into a false sense of security.

It was an amazing gift which Detective Inspector Coleman possessed for turning on his charm whenever he felt the occasion demanded it, and one for which he was well known and envied among his colleagues. The fact that it was completely false never seemed to dawn upon his unfortunate victims until too late; and all the time his brain would be clearly and unscrupulously working out a plan whereby he could trick them into betraying themselves. Such, had she but known it, were his tactics with Thelma now; except in her case it was not herself but somebody else that he sought to make her betray.

'And now, Miss Bancroft,' he began in his most kindly tones, 'I should like you to tell me as briefly as possible all that has happened to you since you went up to bed at — what time was it?'

'Half past eleven.'

And as Benjamin had done before, she proceeded to give a detailed account of all the strange happenings which had come under her notice throughout the night. At the beginning, it agreed with Benjamin's down to the minutest detail. It was only later on that it began to diverge from the strict line of truth; a fact of which the inspector was intuitively conscious, although what actually happened had not so far come under his observation.

When describing how Robert had entered Benjamin's room, Thelma omitted all reference to the attempted murder and testified that she had spoken to him at once, requesting him to leave her father undisturbed and follow her out into the passage; which he did, explaining to her later that the reason for his intrusion had been an important business question he had omitted to ask her father earlier in the evening.

From this point onwards, she returned to the truth again, giving a realistic account of their meeting with Virginia. But when it came to Tony, although she told of his creeping down the stairs, she failed to mention Virginia's explanation of his movements and her admission concerning the clandestine appointment in the lounge. Perhaps the whispered appeal the latter had made to her shortly before she was called had had its effect, for she passed over all these points valiantly; although the tell-tale flush that rose to her cheeks robbed the statement of any authenticity so far as the inspector was concerned. On the other hand, her account of the discovery of the body soon after midnight was accurate to a degree. But when questioned, however, about the quarrel between Robert and Paul, she dismissed it airily as a mere disagreement.

In spite of all this, Coleman was far too clever to let her see that he disbelieved any part of what she had been telling him, and congratulated her, at the conclusion, upon the clearness and precision with which she had answered. Unlike Thelma, he was a past master in the art of deceit; and if it had not been for one rather peculiar action on his part, it would never have occurred to her to doubt him. As it was, directly after complimenting her, he walked across to the door and summoned Sergeant Ridgeway.

'Ask Mr. Harcourt to come over, Sergeant,' he said when that worthy appeared.

Thelma shifted uneasily in her chair. A feeling of panic began to surge up inside her.

The inspector returned to his desk and began studying his notes, apparently having forgotten her presence altogether.

Why did he not tell her to go? Her heart sank as the conviction that he did not believe her began to strengthen. In a few seconds Robert would be here, before she'd had time to let him know what she'd said. And then he'd probably confess, and all her efforts to save him would be set at nought. Or conversely, he might tell a totally different tale, in which case they would both be discredited.

There came a rapping at the door. To Thelma it sounded like her death knell. She was beaten — she could do no more.

180

'Come in!'

The door opened and Robert, pale but determined, entered the room. For a second his eyes met hers, and the warm look of sympathy that passed between them sent a thrill such as he had never known before running wildly through his veins.

'You may leave us now, Miss Bancroft.' The inspector's voice had lost none of its silken persuasiveness.

Scarcely knowing what she was doing, she rose to her feet. At the door she stopped: outside stood the sergeant, holding it open for her. Her hand touched Robert's lightly. And as her fingers met his, he smiled. In spite of the ever-narrowing circle he knew was remorselessly closing around him, he could not resist this spontaneous acknowledgement of her little act of friendliness.

The idea that came to her of whispering a quick warning to him died as she caught the sergeant's steady eye. She passed slowly from the room, leaving behind a nervous but strangely happy Robert to face the wary Inspector Coleman.

10

The Inquiry Continues

Like the other witnesses, Robert was beckoned towards the chair facing the inspector; he obeyed and seated himself, awaiting the expected onslaught.

The inspector started his list of quick-fire questions almost before Robert had time to think how he was going to reply to them. Gone was the suave, sympathetic, paternal man of a few minutes ago, and in his place was a hard and ruthless bully shooting his questions like a machine gun, and seeking to baffle the poor man before him on every possible occasion.

'You're Robert Harcourt?' he snapped at him.

'Yes.'

'You were engaged for some time to Miss Bancroft?'

'Three years.'

'She broke off this engagement a few days ago — why?'

'Because she thought I'd gone to pieces.'

'Drink?'

'Among other things.'

'Almost immediately after breaking with you, she became engaged to the deceased. Were you surprised at this?'

'Naturally. After three years — '

'When did you hear of it?'

'Tonight.'

'Tonight! And what were your feelings? Were you jealous of him?'

'A little. I was more angry than jealous. You see, I didn't think he was the right sort of man for her.'

'Was that the cause of your quarrel with him?'

Robert looked up suddenly. So he knew that already! 'Yes. He said . . . disparaging things about her.'

'And you lost your temper with him — did you assault him?'

Robert looked into the hard, emotionless eyes before him and burst out passionately, 'I nearly strangled him, if that's what you want to know.'

'So I gathered. And now, about this nocturnal call you made — or set out to make — upon Mr. Fredericks. You wanted to see him about a matter of business, didn't you?'

'Business?'

'So you crept quietly up to his room and knocked on the door. You received no answer, so you walked in . . . '

'What are you talking about?'

' . . . and then you came face to face with — '

'Stop!' Robert's nerves could stand no more. The emotions of the night had told upon him more than he thought. 'I'll tell you everything,' he cried. 'But first of all I would have you know that I didn't kill Paul Conway, whatever you may think to the contrary.'

'Then why did you go to Mr. Fredericks' bedroom, uninvited, in the middle of the night?'

'I went to murder Mr. Fredericks.'

'You what?'

'I went expecting to find Mr. Fredericks in that bed. I intended to strangle him!' Robert had risen to his feet; the sweat glistened upon his forehead. At last he was getting his chance to tell the truth! A few seconds elapsed after the delivery of this astounding statement before either of them made any attempt to speak. And when Robert continued, his voice was much more under control.

'I made up my mind to tell you about it, Inspector, before I came into this room,' he said quietly. 'And now I'm going to tell you the whole truth, as God's my judge. And you must either believe it or disbelieve it, as you see fit.' And for the second time that night, he plunged headlong into the amazing narrative that had had its sinister opening only a few hours previously in the black salon of Omar, the fortune teller.

Inspector Coleman listened patiently, making a few notes, and did not interrupt until he reached the point that concerned his meeting with Thelma. 'You say Miss Bancroft did not speak until you had practically got your hands upon her step-father's throat?' he asked him.

'No. Then she cried, 'Stop'.'

'And you did?'

'Yes. It was her voice that brought me to myself.'

The inspector smiled and made a note, while Robert carried on with the vivid account of his adventures. When he had described their meeting with Virginia, Coleman interrupted him again. 'You say she explained her presence at that hour by telling you that she had come to see her father? Did she tell you also why she wished to see him, or if it was a prearranged appointment?'

'She refused to tell us her reason for wishing to see him; and as far as I can remember, we neither of us asked if he was expecting her.'

'And where does Mr. Hargreaves come into all this?'

'Now. I'm just coming to him.' Then and there he proceeded to tell exactly the same story as Thelma had done only a few moments ago. It was evident that Virginia had not been backward in persuading him likewise to suppress the truth. The rest of his story was strictly authentic and led right up to the arrival of the police.

At the conclusion of it, the inspector

looked at him strangely. 'Have you been talking to anybody before you came in here?' he asked suddenly.

'Just one or two remarks to the doctor and Miss Fredericks.'

'Not Miss Bancroft?'

'No. She was too ashamed of me.' His voice became hard as he remembered the stony exterior she had presented to him as they sat awaiting the inspector's summons. But the memory of that brief glance of sympathy she had given him shortly afterwards, and of the exquisite thrill he had experienced at the soft touch of her hand, served to soften his bitterness, and even set the flame of hope quietly burning anew in his heart.

The inspector noted down his last answer, and a scornful little smile flickered at the corners of his lips. 'You say you didn't touch the body, Mr. Harcourt?' His question sounded as cold and impersonal as ever.

'No. I only touched the bedclothes.'

'Do you remember the position of the body?'

'He was lying in bed, slightly on one

side, and quite covered over with the blankets.'

Coleman compared this statement with the one made by the doctor; they tallied exactly, and for the first time during the interview he was puzzled, the truth being the last thing he had expected from Robert.

'You can give us no explanation as to why he came to be in Mr. Fredericks' bed?' he asked.

'None. I was hardly likely to be in his confidence.'

The inspector leant back in his chair with studied carelessness. 'Well, I think that's about all for the present, Mr. Harcourt. And I suggest you go straight up to bed. You must be feeling tired after all your escapades.' The mockery in his voice was so subtle as to be almost unnoticeable. He had no desire to arouse Robert's suspicions — especially now, when he had just begun to see a solution.

'I *am* rather tired.'

'Then the sooner you go, the better.'

'Yes. I'll just say good night to the others first.'

The inspector rose to his feet and crossed to the door. 'Never mind about that, Mr. Harcourt. You take my advice and go now.'

Robert rose to his feet also, and it was only when he met the inspector's steely eye that he realised with a shock that this was no request, but an order. 'Oh!' Without more ado, he felt himself compelled to leave the room and sauntered unwillingly across the hall.

'Sergeant Ridgeway!' The inspector's voice rang out from close behind him as the sergeant sprang to attention. 'Send Miss Fredericks to me.'

Sergeant Ridgeway turned towards the lounge as Robert began slowly mounting the stairs.

With Virginia, Coleman was faced with a problem. He realised this from the moment she entered the room. Here was no innocent, trusting woman to be tricked into admissions, but a cold, determined person with a brain as quick and calculating as his own. When requested to occupy the chair, so easily forced upon the previous witnesses, she declined, saying she

189

preferred to stand. This was the first clash of wills between them, but as their eyes met across the desk, the inspector realised that it would not be the last.

The first thing he asked of her was to give an account of her movements throughout that night. She did so without the slightest hesitation or embarrassment. The inspector received it all in silence. But when she had finished, he looked up. 'And you have no idea as to the reason for Mr. Hargreaves' appearance at all?' he asked.

'None.'

'Even though he was your fiancé and you presumably shared his confidence?'

'I'm convinced he will have some perfectly reasonable explanation for his conduct.'

'You're convinced he *will* have? Have you not asked him for it already, during the hour you've been waiting in the lounge?'

'We haven't discussed it.'

'I see. And Mr. Harcourt? You say you have no idea what he was doing up at so late an hour, either?'

'None whatsoever.'

'In fact, the only person you can account for is Miss Bancroft?'

'And Doctor Prescott.'

'Oh — er — quite. Of course; he heard your screams, didn't he?'

'Yes. His bedroom was close at hand.'

'And what about yourself, Miss Fredericks? What were you doing?'

'I've told you. I had come to see my father.'

'Were you and your father very friendly?'

'Well no, we weren't.'

'Was he expecting you?'

'No.'

'And yet, Miss Fredericks, despite these two facts, you had no qualms about waking him up in the middle of the night. It must have been something very important.'

'It was.'

'Can't you tell me what it was?'

'I'm afraid not.'

Coleman leant back in his chair and looked her full in the eyes. She returned his gaze unflinchingly. 'You're making things very difficult, Miss Fredericks. By withholding knowledge that might be of use to us in our search for the murderer, you may be jeopardising the lives of many innocent people. Not to mention placing yourself in a very unfortunate position.'

'I can't help that.'

'Very well. In that case we shall have to wait until you are asked these questions in court.' He studied her features keenly to note the effect of this final shot. But not by the merest flicker did she convey emotion of any sort other than that of grim determination, which appeared clearly written in every line of her countenance. Seeing this, he acknowledged his defeat. 'That will do, Miss Fredericks,' he said. 'You may return to the lounge.'

He rose and opened the door for her, a faint smile playing about his lips. It was one of Inspector Coleman's nicer qualities that he could accept defeat gracefully. He watched her as she moved across the hall, head erect, regal as a queen, and gave an unwilling sigh of admiration. *What a magnificent creature!* was the thought that ran through his head as she passed into the lounge and disappeared from his sight.

He looked in the direction of the sergeant, who was still keeping to his post of sentry before the lounge door, and making up his mind on the instant he walked across to him. 'You can tell the servants to go to bed. I'll question them in the morning,' he said.

'Very good, sir.'

'See all the outside doors and windows are locked, get the keys, and then keep guard here until I give you further instructions.'

'Yes, sir.' The sergeant clattered over to the servants' stairs and descended until he vanished from view.

Inspector Coleman meanwhile strode briskly forward into the lounge. In front of the fire were Benjamin, the doctor and Thelma — the former apparently in a state of complete nervous exhaustion; while in a far corner of the room were Virginia and Tony, both so intrigued by their own conversation that they did not even notice the inspector's entrance. But his voice soon brought all heads round in his direction.

'Ladies and gentlemen, I wish to

apologise to you all for keeping you up to this unearthly hour.' He stole a glance at Benjamin before proceeding. 'And, most particularly, I should like to offer my apologies to your host.'

A slight murmur of approval broke from Thelma and Doctor Prescott. Once again, with his usual sense of delicacy, Coleman had succeeded in striking just the right note.

'But I trust you will all sympathise with me and realise how necessary it was for me to learn all the facts concerning this tragedy at the earliest possible opportunity,' he continued in the same tone. 'It is for your safety that I have been doing this — for who knows if the murderer of Paul Conway may not be prowling about in our midst at this moment, still on the premises, and it is imperative that the law must be the first to move. But the law cannot move without assistance from you — all of you.' He looked round the circle like an orator taking stock of his audience. 'Until now, you have all been extremely helpful; and that's why I'm anxious for you to place yourselves completely in our hands, and to restrain any irritation you may experience from the harmless formalities to which it is our unfortunate duty to ask you to submit.'

He drew himself up to his full height, his expression immediately changing from kindliness to rugged command. 'Now you will all go to your rooms,' he said, 'with the exception of Mr. Hargreaves, whom I have not yet interrogated — Mr. Harcourt has already retired — and in the morning will hold yourselves in readiness to answer any further questions I may see fit to put to you. No one shall enter or leave the house, and you will regard yourselves as under suspicion for the next twenty-four hours at least. Any evidence you give may be used against you. I trust I make myself clear.'

The last sentence was spoken with a return to his former manner of warm-hearted magnanimity, as though having given his orders and shown his iron hand, he now strove to replace the silken glove. His speech had been received in stony silence, and even when he had concluded it, no burst of frenzied conversation broke from his little band of listeners; but instead, a slight murmur came from the three people by the fire, while Virginia rose, and without another word kissed Tony lightly on the lips and swept imperiously out of the room. After a few seconds the others followed suit, leaving Tony and the inspector to themselves.

'Join me in the study, Mr. Hargreaves,' Coleman instructed.

Slowly and laboriously, supported on either side by his doctor and his beloved step-daughter, Benjamin mounted the staircase. His face, bloodless and almost grey in complexion, looked strained and haggard in the faint illumination from the hall below. The doctor watched him carefully at every step; his look of anxiety increasing as his patient's breathing became more heavy and laboured. His worst suspicions as to the condition of his heart were immediately confirmed. At the first landing they paused for breath.

'You're sure you don't mind sleeping in Paul's room, Father?' Thelma enquired anxiously.

Benjamin looked at her with a gentle

smile. 'Why should I, my dear? We were friends. Paul wouldn't hurt me, even if he could.'

Her eyes flashed angrily, but were instantly flooded with tears.

'Don't cry.'

'It's not him I'm crying for — it's you! I wanted to marry him so as to make you happy, and now — now, I never shall!'

Benjamin pressed her arm tenderly, and without another word being spoken they started ascending the next flight of stairs. They had reached the top and were standing outside the bedroom before she spoke again.

'Good night, Daddy.' She kissed him, then looked up into his poor tired eyes. 'And you do believe what I told you about Robert and the fortune teller, don't you?'

'I don't expect the police will, dear,' he said, smiling. 'But I do.'

At which she held him tightly to her and gave a cry of relief.

'Good night, Prescott.' He gently disengaged himself and opened the door behind him.

'Hadn't I better see you into bed?' the

doctor suggested hastily.

'Certainly not. I'm not dying yet. Look after Thelma. She needs you more than I do.'

Thelma laughed nervously.

'Good night, darling. And don't worry. I'll see what can be done about Robert.'

'Bless you!'

And the door was slowly closed upon them as they turned on their heels and walked back to their bedrooms.

Downstairs in the study, Coleman was proceeding with his interrogation of Tony. Little good did it do him; Tony was not to be shaken by any of the inspector's wiles. He gave his account of all that had happened to him, and not by a hair's breadth did he allow himself to be tricked into contradicting or withdrawing any statement he had made.

In the main he merely corroborated what the others had testified before him, but when asked point-blank for an explanation of his stealthy visit to the lounge in the middle of the night, he resorted to a lie that was neither clever nor convincing. He had dropped one of his cuff links, he explained, and had come down to look for it. And when asked sarcastically whether he had found it, he produced it from his pocket with an air of nonchalance that would not have deceived a babe.

'What time did you retire, Mr. Hargreaves?' the inspector asked him in a final attempt to get at something.

'Some time before twelve, I think. Couldn't say for sure.'

'And it was some time *after* twelve before you discovered that you had lost one of your cuff links?'

'Yes, it must have been.'

'Why are you still fully dressed?'

'I wasn't tired.'

'So you sat up and read a book, I suppose?'

'How did you know, Inspector? I did sit up and read a book. Then, all of a sudden, I began to feel drowsy. So I got up and was just going to get into bed when I noticed one of my cuff links was missing, so I immediately tried to remember where I could have lost it.'

'And the first place you hit upon was the lounge?'

'That's right. So I crept downstairs — '

'In spite of the fact that you had begun to feel drowsy?'

'Oh yes, rather. Woke me up thoroughly, this did — the shock of it, you know. And so I crept downstairs — '

'That'll do!' Coleman was becoming irritated.

'Wait a minute. I haven't got to the exciting part yet.'

'The exciting part?'

'Yes. When I saw the figure running across the lawn. Don't you want me to tell you that?'

'Go ahead!' barked the inspector, a gleam of hope appearing in his eye.

'Well, as I was saying, I crept down the stairs and into the lounge. And just as I got inside, I saw a figure run through the French windows across the lawn in the direction of the west gate.'

'Where's that?'

'Facing the back of the house, about a hundred yards away. It leads out into the road.'

'And what did you do?'

'Well, I began to follow it. But before I

was halfway across the room, I heard screams from upstairs, and then — well then, the next thing I knew, they were all down here in the hall.'

'Have you told anybody else about this?'

'No, I haven't.'

'Good.' The inspector leant forward and studied his notes for some moments in silence. 'You say you heard screams and that almost immediately afterwards you opened the door and found everybody outside in the hall?' he asked slowly.

'Yes, Inspector. That's right.'

'But Mr. Hargreaves, there was quite an appreciable time between those screams and the arrival downstairs of the other occupants in the house — so much time, in fact, that it's rather surprising to find that you didn't hasten upstairs to ascertain the cause of the uproar. Why did you not do this?'

'Well, I didn't like to interfere because I thought they might start asking me questions,' he replied. 'And — well, you see, Inspector, I felt they'd possibly think it pretty strange of me to be wandering about at that time of night — '

'It *was* pretty strange, Mr. Hargreaves.'

'Well, not really, as I'd only come down to find a cuff link; but they might not have understood — '

'You're quite right. I don't expect they would.' The inspector's voice sounded cold and distant, his disbelief at this moment becoming particularly apparent. Realising that he was getting nowhere, he tried to change his tactics. But once again, to his great annoyance, he found himself faced with a brick wall. For Tony appeared to know nothing of his fellow guests, and to care even less. Eventually the inspector gave it up. 'Here was a party of six people besides yourself,' he declared impatiently, 'and you don't seem able to give me a bit of practical information about any one of them — not even your own fiancée.'

'There were seven of them besides me, Inspector,' Tony chipped in unexpectedly.

'Who was the seventh?'

'Mr. Fredericks' brother. He went home at about half past eleven.'

Inspector Coleman sat up with a start.

This was something new; somehow he'd taken it for granted up till now that all the people at the party had stayed the night.

'You're sure he was the only guest we haven't mentioned?' he asked eagerly.

'Oh yes, quite. There weren't any more.'

'Can't you tell me anything about him?'

'Sorry; I only met him for the first time tonight. But Mr. Fredericks might — '

'Come in!' The inspector cut him short, shouting in response to a smart rap from outside.

Sergeant Ridgeway half-opened the door and stuck his head round. 'Police surgeon, sir,' he said.

'Very well. Show him in.'

The door was opened wider as a short, fussy little man entered the room accompanied by Detective Blake. It was possibly his entrance that was responsible for their failure to hear a car starting up, near at hand; the sound of which speedily faded into the distance, dying away before any of them had noticed it.

11

Disappearance

For the next few minutes, the inspector found genuine relief in listening to the short, pedantic sentences of the police surgeon, as a contrast to the irritating vagaries of Tony. Seizing his opportunity, he dismissed the latter the moment the former arrived, sending him to his room with strict instructions that he was to remain there without attempting to communicate with anybody until the morning. With these instructions added to the fact that Sergeant Ridgeway had just received orders to patrol every passage for all the world like a warder, the house presented more the atmosphere of a prison than that of a harmless weekend party, as originally intended.

'Death by strangulation. Time — some few minutes before midnight,' was the police surgeon's verdict.

'Just as I expected.' The inspector had

completely lost his mask of depression, and his whole countenance became wreathed in a seraphic smile. 'You're sure it was a few minutes before midnight and not a few minutes after?' he questioned meticulously.

'Quite sure,' the surgeon replied. 'Only a few minutes, though — possibly about fifteen at the outside.'

'Hm. I see.' The question of minutes was the one thing that worried the inspector, for it was this element of time that made up the sole factor which could spoil his little case. 'And the man died in the position in which he was found, you say? No chance of his having been carried there or anything like that?'

'I don't think so — so far as I can judge without a more thorough examination.'

'Quite. Thank you.'

'And now, if you don't mind, gentlemen, I'll be getting back to my bed.'

'Certainly. Show him out, Blake.'

The two men left the room, and the inspector returned his desk. When Detective Blake returned, he was still perusing his notes.

Blake closed the door and took a few paces into the room. After a second or two, the Inspector raised his head. 'Blake,' he said briskly, 'I believe this is my lucky day. Didn't we clean up the Huntsford jewel robbery this morning, when we ran the whole crowd to earth in that little village?'

'I don't see that was so lucky, though, sir. We'd worked hard enough for it. I think we deserved it.'

'Maybe we did, but it was a stroke of luck that led us to them, all the same. That was the first break we had today. Then came the second: being on the spot, we were detailed for this.'

'Call that luck, sir?'

'Wait a minute! There's number three to come yet. Having been unexpectedly forced into taking up a case that might easily spell promotion for the pair of us, my luck held out even further,' the inspector continued, leaning back in his seat with a satisfied grunt, 'for within little more than a couple of hours after arriving here, I have every reason to believe that I have discovered the murderer of Paul Conway!'

'You don't say!'

'I do. The motive — everything. It's all here. The one thing that worries me at all now is this question of time. The suspect declares that he didn't leave the lounge downstairs until twelve o'clock. Not that he's necessarily speaking the truth, of course, but the two women seem definite in their statements that it was after midnight when they met him; and unless they're all shielding one another, I can't see their object in lying about it.'

'Perhaps one of 'em's in love with him? Wouldn't that account for it, sir?'

'One of them *was* in love with him,' Coleman murmured. 'Perhaps she still is. You never know with women. Of course she must be in love with him, though, or she wouldn't be trying to shield him, would she?' He stroked his chin thoughtfully. 'But then there's the other — Miss Fredericks. I can't see why she should lie about the time too. Of course, she's behaved most curiously the whole way through; refusing to answer questions and being as difficult as she could. She'd probably lie just for the pure devilment of it.'

'And who's the man, sir?'

'Mr. Robert Harcourt, the good-looking young chap standing close to Mr. Fredericks when we arrived. Motive: jealousy — his fiancée had thrown him over for the deceased. They'd had a row previously, earlier in the evening. And the woman — Miss Bancroft, the fair one — knows he did it, and she's shielding him; possibly realised she's in love with him as soon as he came up against it. And her father — the old man, Mr. Fredericks — he's been trying to keep his name out of it too. Shouldn't be surprised if he's an accomplice. Anyway, we'd better keep our eyes on those two birds, all the time. They mustn't get together, whatever happens, or they'll be thinking out some alibi. That's why I've got the sergeant patrolling all the passages. As long as we can keep them apart, so not one of them knows what evidence the other is giving, we'll have them on toast. And unless I'm very much mistaken, tomorrow will bring forth some astonishing confessions from them both.'

'Can't we get him on fingerprints, sir?' suggested Blake cautiously.

'Not a hope.' The inspector shook his head. 'He discovered the body, so he's a perfectly good excuse for having his fingerprints plastered all over it. But I'll get him in spite of that, never you fear. He told me a crazy story tonight about a fortune teller and being hypnotised and all sorts of stuff that sounded as though he'd taken it out of some lurid detective story. But I've got it all down, and tomorrow I'm going to have that pretty story of his all over again, word by word; and if it differs by a hair's breadth from what he's been telling me tonight . . . well, we'll know the whole thing's a fake, and I'll get the truth out of him.'

'How about the woman, though — Miss, er, Bancroft? Did she spill this crazy tale too?'

'No, she didn't. They're evidently not on the best of terms at the moment. I think her story's phoney too, although it certainly didn't agree with his.'

'Sounds a pretty clear case to me then,' Blake declared optimistically.

'Dead clear! You take it from me. Tomorrow morning we'll have that young man just where we want him, and maybe the old one too, although I'm not worrying about him because he's pretty far gone already.'

'Far gone, sir?'

'Ill. He's not long for this life; you look into his eyes. They'll tell you all you want to know.'

'How about the other young man, sir? Is he all right?'

'Tony Hargreaves, you mean? Well, now you're asking something, Blake. Seems that he and Miss Fredericks are quite another case; they don't fit in with this one at all. I can't quite make out whether they're being deliberately tantalising, or whether there's something more behind it. It's his story of losing his cuff link that gets me. Of course it's obviously faked, but what's his motive? And then again, there's that figure he says he saw.'

'A figure, sir?'

'Yes. He claims to have seen a figure that ran out through the French windows as he came into the lounge.'

'That's interesting, sir, if he's not making it up.'

'Quite. But then he goes on to say that he couldn't follow it because at that moment he was attracted by the sound of voices from the hall, and going out to them he was told about the murder, which put the whole affair clean out of his mind. But there again, it's quite plain he's been lying.'

'Why, sir? I don't see that,' said Blake in a puzzled tone.

'Well, according to the time he left his room to go downstairs, as testified by three witnesses — which, by the way, was about five minutes before the discovery of the murder — several minutes must have elapsed between the time he entered the lounge and the arrival of the others in the hall. All of which gave him ample opportunity either to raise an alarm or to follow the figure himself, both of which he failed to do. Therefore there is only one fact to be deducted from that.'

'He was trying to keep his presence secret, sir?'

'Precisely. Therefore, the story of the

cuff link is completely false. For if it had been something as easily explainable as that, there would have been no object in holding back. But there's one thing about the story that interests me all the same.'

'What, sir?'

'It's that figure which he claims to have seen . . . ' He consulted his notes, ' . . . running in the direction of the west gate. Now, if only we could trace that, we might — '

'Been raining too heavily to find any footprints, sir.'

'Yes. I was afraid of that.'

At this point the conversation was interrupted by a violent battering at the door, and before Coleman had time to answer it, a wild figure had staggered headlong over the threshold. It was the normally slow-moving Sergeant Ridge-way; but before the inspector had time to frame any question, the sergeant sought in broken, breathless sentences to explain his unceremonious intrusion.

'Sorry, sir,' he gasped, 'but something's 'appened!'

'Well?' the inspector snapped impatiently.

'It's the doctor, sir — 'e's gone — run away. I found 'is door open a minute ago and came down to tell you.'

'I thought I told you to patrol those passages for the remainder of the night!' the inspector shouted at him.

'Yes, sir. But — '

'Why didn't you do as you were told? Come on, Blake!' And he rushed out of the room followed by Blake, leaving a red-faced and embarrassed sergeant behind him.

Upstairs on the first floor, they found everything as the sergeant had told them. The door of the doctor's room stood wide open, while the occupant, to all intents and purposes, appeared to have vanished.

'Keep as quiet as you can,' the inspector hissed into Blake's ear as they entered the room together. 'We don't want to rouse the house, if we can help it.'

They crept inside cautiously and looked about. The light was still burning, and it took only a few seconds to convince them that nobody was there. This done, they moved over to the bed, where a brief glance told them that it had not been slept in. Everything seemed in perfect order: the straight-backed chairs, the dressing-table, the washstand, all perfectly ordinary. It was very cold.

Blake shivered. 'It's that window! It's open!'

They hurried over to the window, the curtains billowing out in the breeze. The inspector put his head out. 'No chance of his having escaped this way,' he said almost at once, drawing back into the room again. For the side of the house presented a smooth surface of unbroken creeper.

'Then how the deuce did he get out?' demanded Blake in a baffled whisper.

'Probably through the front door — I expect he did it while the sergeant was patrolling the floor above.'

Halfway down the stairs, the inspector stopped and pointed. 'What did I say?' he declared triumphantly. The front door stood wide open.

At the foot of the stairs was the sergeant. He came forward to meet them, the guilty expression on his countenance even more pronounced than before. 'I've just discovered, sir, that the front door is — '

'Open. We know.' He turned to Blake. 'Know where the garage is?'

'No, sir. Afraid I don't.'

'We'll go and find out. Sergeant, you stay here. Blake, come with me outside.'

In a few minutes, aided by the sergeant's torch, they had found the garage, which was situated only about ten yards from the front door, opening onto the drive. The inspector shone the torch back onto the path again. This time his efforts were rewarded; fresh tyre marks showed up against the wet surface. He went forward and tried the large double doors — padlocked!

'You're good at locks, Blake.'

'Force it, sir?'

The only reply was a curt nod, and in a few seconds the doors were opened wide. With the aid of the torch, they found the electric light switch, and there was revealed to their gaze a large and extremely tidy garage with room enough for at least half a dozen cars — Benjamin evidently had given plenty of thought to his weekend parties when it was being constructed. But at the moment there were not more than two cars standing before them.

Coleman jumped onto the running board of one of them and flashed his torch inside. 'Miss Bancroft's,' he announced. He did the same with the next. 'Miss Fredericks'. Now, where's the third? Fredericks must have one. That's what the doctor's gone off in, I should think.'

'Unless he has one of his own.'

'We'll have to check up on that at once. Not Fredericks himself, in the state he's in. Wake up the butler — he'll know.'

'Okay. And then shall I ring up the station, sir?'

'Never mind that. You find out about the cars first.'

The inspector followed back to the house at a more leisurely rate, his brain intent upon this new problem. Reaching the front door, he peered into the hall and beckoned Sergeant Ridgeway towards him. 'Sergeant, for the rest of the night you remain on guard outside the house, and see you do it more efficiently than you did inside.'

'Yes, sir.' The sergeant hurried off into the darkness, only too glad to get off so lightly.

As he was about to enter the study, the inspector was confronted by Blake and the nervous figure of Parker, who had been unceremoniously dragged out of bed, and now stood shivering in the cold, damp air.

'I haven't done anything, sir — honest I haven't!' he whimpered piteously as his frightened eyes passed from one to the other of them.

'That's all right,' Coleman put in roughly, 'we only want to ask you a few questions. Tell me — is Doctor Prescott a frequent visitor here?'

'Why yes, sir; he's the master's oldest friend.'

'And does he usually come by car or train?'

'Train, sir. He says he gets enough of his car during the week and likes to be thoroughly rural, as he terms it, when he comes down here.'

'I see. Now can you remember, Parker, whether he arrived by train this afternoon as usual? Or did he bring his car, by way of a change?'

'He came by train, sir,' Parker asserted definitely.

'Why are you so sure?'

'Because I saw him coming up the drive, sir. It was late in the afternoon, and Miss Bancroft had asked me to walk down to the gates and see if any of the guests were in sight.'

'Right. Now just one thing more. Can you remember if Mr. Fredericks came home in his car tonight?'

'I'd be ready to swear he did, sir. I remember hearing it coming up the drive when I was in the kitchen, and saying to Cook — 'Why, there's the master at last; won't Miss Thelma be pleased!' You see, he was a bit late, sir, and — '

'So in all there were three cars belonging to the family?'

'Yes, sir.'

'Can you remember the number and make of Mr. Fredericks' car?'

'Yes, sir. A Daimler, number YW7556.'

'Colour?'

'Black. Four-seater, saloon.'

'Thanks. Got all that down, Blake?'

'Yes, sir.'

Coleman's reliable assistant had stood by with notebook and pencil throughout the entire interview.

'And now before you go, Parker, just tell us your own personal opinion of Doctor Prescott, will you?'

'But, sir, I — a guest — '

'Do you like him?'

Parker pulled himself together. 'Yes, sir, I do. He's one of the finest gentlemen I've ever met. And if you ask any of the other servants, they'll tell you exactly the same.'

'Thanks. That's all I wanted to know. Good night, Parker. You can go back to bed now.'

When Parker had gone, Coleman turned to the puzzled-looking Blake. 'Guess you thought that last question of mine was a bit irregular,' he said with a forced laugh, 'but it's one of the best ways of finding out what you want to know about a man's character. Don't ask his friends; ask the people who wait upon him.'

'And what have you gathered from it, sir?'

'Nothing! He merely put into words what I felt when I interviewed him.'

'Pretty definite that he's made off with the old man's car, though.'

'Yes, but I can't understand why. You'd better ring up the station now: usual procedure; give him the number and a description of the car, and they can get on to the Yard and warn all stations to keep a look out for him.'

He flung himself into his chair impatiently as Blake crossed to the telephone and earned out his instructions. As he replaced the receiver, Coleman began to talk again. 'It must have been something he saw through that window that made him run away. What was it he saw? That's something that he alone can tell us.'

He relapsed into a moody silence as Blake closed his notebook sharply and asked, 'What about patrolling the passages, sir? The sergeant was doing it, but now he's stationed outside — '

'You do it, then, Blake. Lock them all in this time. I don't intend to have any more disappearances tonight. And give a good look to make sure they're all there before you do it.'

'Yes, sir.' And having received his orders, Blake quietly withdrew, leaving the inspector to his uncomfortable speculations.

The clock in the hall chimed half past three; the house was silent as the grave. Out in the darkness, messages were being speedily transmitted from station to station, village policemen were being warned to keep their eyes skinned — and somewhere hiding in the blackness of the night was a poor white-haired old man; and a car was being driven recklessly in defiance of justice!

12

Locked In

Robert Harcourt ascended the stairs towards his bedroom, in accordance with the instructions of Inspector Coleman. He entered his room and, without switching on the light, threw himself full-length upon the bed, sunk in the depths of despair.

Lying there in the darkness, he went over the events of the evening incident by incident and in conclusion was forced to admit himself baffled. The whole thing seemed like some fantastic hallucination — the vain imaginings of a drunkard.

Despite of the outlandishness of it all, something at the back of his mind told him repeatedly that it was all true. The black room, the fortune teller, the crystal, the command to kill — all had really happened, and only a few hours ago.

At last, when darkness threatened to

engulf him altogether, one point became suddenly clear, and he realised that everything rested upon its verification. Who had first put the idea of the fortune teller into his head? And when? Somebody must have told him about Omar, and told him many times too, otherwise why should he have felt his visit there had been ordained as an important part in the furtherance of some scheme? Why couldn't he remember the time or the place he had been told? And how had he come to write the address down himself, without having the slightest remembrance of doing so? Answer those questions and he felt he would be a long way towards solving the mystery, and setting his mind at rest as to the part he had so unknowingly played in it.

He remembered drinking a lot during the afternoon, and he recalled quite easily conversations he'd had and the places he'd been to; but from the moment he left the club behind Shaftesbury Avenue and was seized upon with the notion of visiting the fortune teller, everything slipped back into that haze of unreality.

It was then he was seized upon by the

most ghastly suspicion of all. As he lay stretched out there in the darkness, he began to suspect himself of being a murderer! So lost to the present did he become amid this deep sea of horror, that he failed to hear the shout of surprise from the sergeant as he discovered the room next door bereft of its occupant.

Next came the clatter of footsteps as Blake and Coleman rushed upstairs to ascertain the truth of what had been told them. But this passed him by unnoticed also, as did their retreating and slightly quieter footsteps when they returned down the stairs again. Not one sound of all this entered his distorted brain.

A few minutes after these had died away, however, there came the sound of the door of his room being carefully opened and closed again, and the subsequent feeling that someone was in the room with him, which somehow brought his senses back to normal. He didn't move, but waited, tense in every limb. Gradually a fragrant perfume wafted across to him; and it only needed the soft feminine voice to convince him of what he scarcely dared hope to be true.

'Robert, are you awake? Can I talk to you?'

The sound of her voice was sufficient to bring him instantly to his feet. 'Of course.' He came over to her and stretched out his hand.

'Don't switch on the light,' she said quickly, sensing what he was about to do. They stood facing one another closely; he could feel her warm breath against his cheeks as she spoke. 'You know why I've come?'

'I — I think I do, Thelma.' She took a step nearer to him — their bodies were now pressed against each other — and raised her face to his.

'Do you know, now?'

Her proximity to him, the soft warmth emanating from her body, the fragrance that filled his nostrils, and the tentative touch of her mouth against his, all lifted him from deepest hell to the most unbelievable paradise.

After their lips had met and clung together for several seconds in a passionate embrace, he gently released her. 'You do believe me then?' he said, still scarcely daring to credit his good fortune.

'I did all the time, darling,' she replied. 'Only I — I was stupid. I'm so sorry, Robert.'

Her face felt moist, and he gently lifted his hand to brush away the tears from her soft warm cheeks. 'Darling,' he pleaded with the utmost tenderness, 'please don't cry. Here, let's sit down.' He led her towards the bed where, still clasped in each other's arms, they sat down. Gradually her sobs grew less frequent and stopped. 'There,' he said, as he took his handkerchief and lightly dabbed her eyes. 'All over?'

'All over.' She smiled. 'I don't think I ever appreciated you properly before. Oh, darling, I do love you so much.'

'You — don't know — how you've relieved me, Thelma,' he said haltingly. 'I don't know what I should have done if you hadn't believed me. I — I'd almost begun to disbelieve in myself.'

'What do you mean, dear?'

'Well, my story sounded so improbable that, lying here alone, I began to think that perhaps I really had done it after all. But I couldn't have done it, Thelma, could I?'

'Of course not, my dear.'

'I'm afraid nobody else believes me, though.'

'Father does, I think. I told him the whole story and he said he'll do everything in his power to help you. That sounds as though he does, doesn't it?'

'Yes, but I wish I could make the inspector believe it.'

'The inspector?' There was a slight catch in her voice. 'Did you tell him — the truth?'

'Why yes, of course. It seemed the only thing to do.'

He was surprised at her question; still more so when she went on: 'Of course, darling; it was the only thing to do. But — but I'd told them something quite different. You see, when I came to tell them about you, I suddenly realised what a dreadful position you were in, and how much I — I loved you, and so I told him that I spoke to you as soon as you entered Father's bedroom and — and that I had persuaded you to come away without disturbing him.'

'But what was I supposed to be doing there, then?'

'You'd come to see him about some business you'd forgotten to discuss, earlier in the evening.'

Robert groaned. 'Oh God, now I understand what he was getting at when he shot all those questions at me. He doesn't believe either of us. And now you're in it too!'

'I was in it, darling, without that. He never asked me what I was doing in Father's bedroom myself.'

'I don't understand.'

'I suppose the fact that he never put it to me was because he'd disbelieved me from the start.'

God, would this thing never end; this terrible mystery which seemed to be slowly gathering them all into its net? Now Robert's apprehensions were not only for himself but for her also.

As though she were unconsciously carrying on his train of thought she added: 'Father feels that they suspect him too. You see, he tried to shield you, and the Inspector seemed to see through it.'

Robert gave a mirthless laugh; it was all getting beyond him.

'It seems about the only people left are Virginia and Tony,' he observed sarcastically. 'Or do you think they suspect them too?'

'I shouldn't be surprised . . . By the way, did Virginia ask you not to mention about Tony going down to the lounge to meet her?'

'Yes. I promised I wouldn't.'

'I did, too. I wonder why she wanted it kept secret?'

'Ask me another!'

'After you came up here I was sitting in the lounge, and when Virginia came back after seeing the inspector, I happened to overhear some of their conversation. They kept saying something about 'being in it together'. Then he asked her if she'd decided to tell him her secret yet, and she said no. It was at that moment the inspector came in.'

'So you heard no more?'

'No. But I wonder if it's all connected

in some way with her reason for wanting to call on Father. You remember how she refused to explain that when we asked her?'

'Yes. But she wasn't the only one. Thelma, darling, I know the Inspector didn't ask you that leading question, but may I put it to you now? Tell me why you went to your father's room tonight?'

She turned her head and faced him. 'It was to discuss you, and the advisability of my marrying — or not marrying — Paul.'

'Now I understand.'

'We'd been discussing it downstairs, and were going to do so again after breakfast in the morning. But Father came to my room and said he'd a new idea and would like to have it out with me at once; so — '

'You went along to his room, found him asleep — '

'Heard somebody coming, slipped behind the curtain — '

'And found it was me. So that was your little secret?'

'Yes. Silly, wasn't it?'

'Well, we all seem to be in it one way or

another — except the doctor, of course. I expect he's come out all right.'

Thelma looked at him in amazement. 'The doctor?' she repeated. 'Why, haven't you heard? He's run away! That's what all the noise was about. I peeped into his room before I came to you, and he'd gone!'

'Doctor Prescott! The one person who seemed completely above suspicion of any kind. What on earth can it mean?'

'Did you hear a car outside some time ago?' she asked suddenly, going off on a tangent. He shook his head. 'I did. Quite clearly; as though it were being started up in the garage. I didn't pay much attention to it at the time, but that must have been the Doctor — he must have taken somebody's car. Father's, Virginia's or mine . . . Ssh!' She broke off suddenly. 'Listen!'

Out of the distance came the noise of footsteps. Nearer and nearer they came, until suddenly they stopped and there was a faint click.

'Quick,' Thelma whispered, 'get into the bed!'

And before he could reply, she'd vanished into the darkness. Hastily he scrambled into bed and buried his head in the pillow, forcing himself to close his eyes. He was only just in time, for the next instant the door was softly opened and the ray from a torch travelled unerringly toward the bedstead. Only for a second did it rest upon his face, before it was extinguished and the door closed as softly as it had been opened.

Again there was a silence: then a tell-tale click as the lock shot home. Throwing back the bedclothes he jumped to his feet, blindly stretching out his arms until he sensed again the fragrant perfume, and closed them about the body of the woman he loved.

'I was hiding behind the door,' she whispered with a slight giggle. 'Wasn't it lucky I heard them coming?'

'But your room! When they check before locking you in, they'll see you're not — '

'Oh no, they won't — they'll only glance round quickly as they did here. And I've left the bed quite well disguised with the pillow in it. I guessed I might be here for a long time, so I took a few precautions.'

She rose gently to her feet and took hold of his hands: 'Let's go and sit by the window,' she whispered, 'we can be more comfortable there.'

They reached the cushioned window seat, and sinking down upon them she let her head nestle against his shoulder.

Almost unconsciously he raised his disengaged hand and pulled aside one of the heavy curtains; a faint, straggling shaft of moonlight broke into the room. The storm had gone for the moment, but the angry clouds and the deep blackness of the night foretold for it an early return.

'Thelma!' His eye travelled towards the locked door. 'Tomorrow — what about the morning?'

'Tomorrow?' she repeated in a tone drowsy with happiness. 'Why not be content with tonight?'

The curtains came to and darkness took possession of the room; but even this seemed to vibrate curiously with the strong intensity of their passion.

13

Escape

It was now nearly a quarter to four, and a heavy silence reigned over everything. Against the blackness of the night, the house stood out in ragged silhouette, only one light burning in the study window. This cast a faint radiance across the gravel drive, to be almost immediately defeated by the close shadows clinging to the spruce hedges which skirted it on either side.

The light was serving to make it possible for the still wakeful Inspector Coleman to consult his notes at regular intervals, interspersed with grunts indicative of thought as he added fresh notes to the already carefully filled pages.

One conclusion became ever clearer in his mind with the passing of the hours: namely Robert's guilt. It required all his strength of will to prevent him from mounting the staircase to that young man's room and submitting him to an immediate interrogation, without further ado.

But, he realised, his method of approach must be something more subtle. Unfortunately for him, however, he had underrated Robert's powers of perception and was under the delusion that the former fully believed his story had been accepted for gospel truth; hence his belief the morning would be the best time for pursuing the enquiry. Safe in a fool's paradise, thought the inspector, Robert would go to bed; and then, without the least warning, he could pounce upon him. With the shock of this, with his confidence thus abruptly shattered, who knew what he might be led into confessing?

The inspector rubbed his hands in joyful anticipation of the morrow, and cast impatient glances towards the clock on the mantelpiece.

★ ★ ★

Outside in the cold stood another person for whom the passing of time seemed

interminable. This was Sergeant Ridgeway.

His tour round the house consisted of
marching down one side of the curving
drive, through a little gate on the left,
round the side of the house and through
the kitchen garden, past the French
windows leading out from the lounge,
finally passing through another little gate
on to the other side of the drive and so
proceeding back to where he had
originally started from.

Any interest this held for him waned
all too soon. Then, with great daring,
considering what had happened already,
he decided to keep to the drive and the
front of the house altogether, thus leaving
the back and sides to look after
themselves.

At one end of the drive stood the police
car in which the three of them had
arrived. To the sleepy Sergeant pacing
monotonously up and down, it presented
all that his tired legs and still more tired
brain could desire — and finally, after a
cautious glance to see that neither the
inspector nor Detective Blake was in

sight, he crept into its darkened interior, where with a sigh of infinite relief, he sank back among its old but still soft cushions.

It was not long before the demon sleep sought to get him into its grip; and as warmth had begun to slowly steal over his body, he felt it harder to resist than he had out in the open air. Finally he gave up the struggle altogether and sank into a deep slumber.

In a few minutes his heavy breathing bore noisome witness to the fact that he was fast asleep. Poor Sergeant Ridgeway, the typical village 'bobby', who for years had dozed so peacefully upon his beat! He was too old to change his habits now — murder or no murder!

The sergeant thus disposed of, things immediately began to happen. His retreat into the police car, although unnoticed by his superiors, had not been so completely overlooked by somebody else; and it was that somebody who could now have been seen creeping out onto a windowsill on the top floor and after a second's indecision slowly clambering down the drainpipe. So surreptitiously was this performed that it might have passed unchallenged, had not Thelma and Robert still been sitting in their window-seat. Robert was amazed when, on drawing back the curtains once again to look out, he saw a pair of legs slowly sliding down the drainpipe by the side of the window.

His sudden intake of breath caused Thelma to look out also. She was flabbergasted; not only by the fact that somebody should be directly disobeying the inspector's instructions that nobody was to leave the house, but mainly by the discovery that the extremely well-shaped pair of legs before them were those of a woman! It hardly required a glance at the tense, set face that followed to convince them both of their first suspicion.

Robert drew back the curtain further, and now the female figure was below them, already almost indistinguishable in the gloom. By flattening their faces against the glass, they could just make her out, and note that she was dressed in a heavy overcoat and small, tight-fitting hat;

a few seconds later she had reached the ground.

The moment her feet touched the earth, Virginia — for it was she — without the slightest hesitation, turned and ran nimbly down the drive. To the two watchers above, her destination was obvious — the garage! Hence the heavy overcoat and the gauntlet gloves she now produced from her pocket as she ran. Reaching it, she opened the door and disappeared within.

'She's going to try to get away in her car,' Thelma said. 'But it's broken down.'

'We've got to stop her,' Robert cried. 'We can't tell the police, but we ought to do something about it. They're sure to find out in the morning, and then she'll be under suspicion. They'll scour the country for her — might even accuse her of committing the murder.'

'And they might be right! All this secrecy about her meeting with Tony; and now she's trying to run away. She must have some reason for making such a desperate attempt as this, mustn't she?'

'Yes, I suppose she must. But surely

you don't believe she's a murderer, Thelma?'

'Of course not,' she relented softly, 'but I believe she knows who is.'

'Then why didn't she tell the police?'

'Perhaps she did.'

'That's not very likely, or she wouldn't be trying to get away now.'

'Virginia's a strange woman, Robert. She's an enigma to me just as she is to Father. What she does in London, who her friends and interests are, neither of us know. But one thing I do know — Virginia would never run away from anything to save her own skin. If she's running away tonight, it's to save somebody else's. To save them, or else to warn them!'

'To warn them? That's an idea.'

Robert rose to his feet and began pacing up and down. 'I think you're right about Virginia — if she gets away from this house tonight, she must have some definite goal; some definite person she desires to see — perhaps someone whom she desires to warn. In which case she must be followed, if for no other reason than for her own safety. Now, your car is

240

in the garage and — '

'Robert!' There was genuine anguish in her voice. 'You're not going to — ?'

'Yes, my dear, I am. With your permission, I'm going to follow her.'

'With my permission?'

'Yes. You see, if I don't get back here first thing in the morning, it's going to be rather nasty for you trying to explain, I mean. And so — '

Thelma laughed. 'I'll give you my permission, Robert, on one condition: that you take me with you! Is it agreed?'

'But Thelma, you must be sensible about this. Why, I might have to follow her all through the night. And I don't even know whether we should be safe from physical violence. Anything might happen! And there's the police to think of too — supposing they were to find out that we'd disappeared? What conclusion would they come to? Then there's your father . . . What would his position be when the one and only person he loves has deserted him? Tell me that?'

'My father would never want me to do anything I felt to be wrong,' came her definite reply. 'When the man I'm in love with is going into danger, there is only one thing for me to do, and that's to go with him. And don't try to put me off by saying I should be in the way, because you don't believe that any more than I do.'

'All right. You win!'

He opened the window again and leant out. Cautiously, with his hand he tested the drainpipe down which Virginia had recently descended; as far as he could judge it seemed perfectly firm. He drew back into the room.

'There's only one way of getting down to the drive, and that's by the drainpipe — the same as Virginia did. Think you can manage that?'

'Of course I can, darling.'

'Very well, then. You'll want a coat of some kind,' he said, as she shivered slightly, more from excitement than coldness. 'You'd better have mine. I'll wear my mac. And we'd better take some of these blankets along to cover ourselves up with; it'll be pretty icy driving on a night like this.'

And with her help, he stripped several

of the blankets from the bed.

At last three or four blankets and the overcoat were piled up together on the window-seat, and she was helping him into his mac.

'Better not put on the coat until you get down there,' he explained, 'as it's so large it might get in your way.'

So it was arranged that he should go down first, and she should throw him down the overcoat and blankets, and then follow herself.

A few seconds later he was descending the drainpipe. The descent proved only a matter of about twenty feet and the going fairly easy. At last his feet touched earth, and he cast a hasty glance around to see if anybody was watching. Satisfied that he was still unobserved, he looked up and waved his hand. A second later his overcoat came hurtling through the air. He caught it; next came the blankets, and then the slender figure of Thelma appeared, climbing steadily down the drainpipe above him.

Without faltering once, she reached the ground and stood beside him.

Carrying the blankets and the overcoat they crept — Thelma leading the way — down the drive, and forced their way through a gap in the hedge into the dark shadows beyond.

It was very cold, and before they went any further, Robert insisted in tense whispers that she should put on his overcoat. She complied only too willingly, and when he helped her on with it a sudden thought struck him:

'Your clothes! I could have sworn you were in pyjamas when I saw you in the study.'

'I was, but when I got to my bedroom and realised the odds were heavily in favour of my being up for the rest of the night, I dressed again to keep myself warm.'

They caught each other's eyes and smiled; but almost immediately the smiles faded from their faces. Time was passing. They must get down to it.

'Before we go any further,' Robert whispered, 'I think I'd better take a look into the garage and see how Virginia's getting on with those repairs of hers.

Then, the moment she gets her car out into the drive, we can slip into yours and be after her at once. If anything goes wrong with your car, we might as well give the whole thing up. She'll have a pretty good start as it is.'

'Yes, but remember it's a straight road whichever way she goes. That ought to help us a little.'

'Okay, you stay here while I have a look around.'

'Wait.' She slipped something into his hand. 'Take this gun. Father gave it to me some years ago, when we went abroad together. I thought we might be needing it.'

Slipping the little automatic into his mackintosh pocket, he crept towards the hedge. He put his head through and was just preparing to follow with the rest of his body, when he stopped quite still as though turned to stone.

He and Thelma were not the only unauthorised people walking about the garden that night. Another person was present; a man in a heavy overcoat and turned-down hat who was also creeping surreptitiously towards the garage. It was the object he was holding in his hand that was most significant to the man who stood watching him. For even at that distance, Robert had detected the shape of a revolver!

After this first shock had worn off, Robert climbed noiselessly through the opening in the hedge and stood back in the shadows as the other passed within a few inches of him, but even so it was not possible to distinguish his features. Giving the man a slight start of him, Robert turned and followed in his footsteps. His unknown quarry had reached the garage door; one hand stretched out to open it while the other still grasped the revolver and raised it, as though preparing to take aim. It was at this moment that Robert acted, and brought the butt of his revolver down with all his might upon the man's unguarded head. He swayed for a moment, gave a gasp, and sank to the ground. The revolver clattered on down the drive.

Robert remained where he was, fearing that Virginia might have heard the noise. But after a few minutes, as nothing happened, he dodged past the thin line of light shining through the opening between the garage doors, and retrieved the revolver; then taking his prostrate victim firmly underneath the arms, he dragged him backwards through the gap in the hedge.

Thelma ran forward to meet him. Then she caught sight of the limp figure on the ground: 'What on earth — who is it?'

'I don't know — a man I saw on the drive,' he explained hurriedly. 'Had a revolver; trying to get into the garage . . . Wait — he's got a torch in his pocket. Now!' He pressed the switch, and a white beam cut its way through the darkness. 'Well I'm damned!'

Looking up at them, with an expression of characteristic fatuity, were the pale features of Tony Hargreaves!

Out went the light on the instant, as they gently lowered him on to the ground.

'Poor old Tony,' said Thelma sympathetically, while Robert knelt down to attend to his injuries.

'I hope nobody saw that light,' he whispered as his fingers touched a huge bump on his unfortunate victim's head.

But he need not have worried. Back in the police car, the sergeant's snores grew louder than ever.

14

Exodus

The light still burned in the study window; Virginia worked on feverishly in the garage; the sergeant turned slightly on one side in his sleep and grunted; while behind the bushes, only a few feet away, Thelma and Robert made ineffectual efforts to bring Tony to.

The most frenzied was the woman in the garage. Clever with her tools though she was, this job was proving tough. Time and again she glanced at Thelma's car, indignation rising as she remembered once again that it was locked. It would take as long to tamper with that as to mend her own car. And so she worked on with tense, nervous concentration, quite unaware of all that had transpired outside the garage. Desperately she applied herself to her task afresh, straining at her eyes in her efforts to concentrate under the beam of one of the headlights.

'And what possible motive can Virginia have in doing this?' thought Robert as he applied a handkerchief dipped in rainwater to Tony's injured head.

His conjecture was cut short by a groan from Tony; at last he was coming to! He opened his eyes and tried to sit up. But a stabbing pain in his temples caused him to flop back quickly. At first Robert and Thelma imagined that he had fainted again. But a few seconds later he opened his eyes once more, and as soon as he saw their faces it was evident from his expression that he remembered the whole thing.

'Feeling bad, Tony?' Thelma inquired in a sympathetic whisper.

'Bad enough,' he said, gingerly feeling the bump on his head. 'Tell me, which of you was it who gave me this?'

'Afraid it was me, Tony. I didn't recognise you. I thought you were a stranger, and when I saw you creeping towards the garage with a revolver in your hand, I followed you and — '

'Dotted me one?'

'Afraid so. But how was I to know it

was you? What are you doing down here, anyway?'

'Me?' his victim cried indignantly. 'What are you doing down here? Here you both are, hiding behind bushes in the early hours of the morning — Thelma with you too, and then — ow!'

For a moment he closed his eyes, while Thelma and Robert exchanged swift, meaning glances. Her eyes seemed to say, 'Go on; tell him.'

Robert could never seriously suspect Tony of anything, in spite of the revolver and the strange circumstances surrounding him, so he quickly explained their position to him.

When he had finished, Tony asked pointedly: 'And may I ask how Thelma came to be in your room?'

'She came to see me to — to talk things over, and one of those damn fool detectives locked us in. Now can you explain your presence here?'

'For the same reason as you two. I saw Virginia out of my window, and thought I'd better follow. You know, protective instinct and all that sort of thing. And so, when I found I was locked in, I just clambered out onto the old ivy. Tough stuff, ivy, you know. And then I was just trailing her to the garage when your boyfriend sloshed me one.'

'But what about the revolver?' his assailant demanded somewhat unsympathetically.

'Just a little practical joke, to frighten her a bit. Stop her slinking off in the early hours again. I keep one handy. Always on the safe side is my motto.'

'What work is it that you do, may I ask, that necessitates the use of a revolver?' Robert frowned.

'No, you may not.' Tony sat up slowly. 'My job has got nothing to do with it.'

'Now listen, Tony,' Thelma said. 'We think Virginia has a special motive in trying to run away like this; she wouldn't go to all this trouble for herself.'

'You think she's shielding somebody else?'

'Yes. And if this is the case, surely it's better to let her get away and follow her?'

'In the hope that she'll lead you to the murderer?'

'Exactly. Don't you think there's something in it?'

'Possibly,' Tony admitted at length. 'But where do I come in now that you've found me? I don't fancy the idea of climbing back up the ivy.'

'Then you must come with us.'

This sudden invitation, much to Thelma's surprise, came from Robert. He had spied a quick, intelligent gleam in Tony's eye whilst Thelma had been explaining things to him, a brisk note that had subsequently crept into his voice. These things, infinitesimal in themselves, were sufficient to prove to him that Tony was not nearly such a fool as he usually appeared. Here was a man who might prove very useful to them.

'Right. I'll come with you,' Tony replied. 'That is, if I can stand,' he added shakily as he attempted to rise.

'No need to do that yet, Tony,' cautioned Thelma, laying her hands gently on his shoulders. 'I'll stay with you while Robert goes to see how Virginia's getting on.'

'That's what you were going to do

when you came across me, I suppose?'

'Yes,' Robert said, rising to his feet. 'Now you do as Thelma says and stay here.'

With little difficulty, Robert once again found his way through the hedge and onto the drive. This time he was allowed to continue his slow progress towards the garage unmolested. He soon arrived at the doors, which were still slightly open, the thin shaft of light striking across his path in the darkness. He peered through the open space. Then as his eyes became accustomed to the faint illumination, he made out the figure of Virginia.

She was standing on the running-board of her car, her back towards him, and she was putting back the tools! The repairs had been completed and in a few seconds she would be in the driving-seat. The car would be backing out of the garage doors, and the moment they had been waiting for would have arrived!

He turned and moved back in the direction whence he had come, as speedily and softly as possible. On his return, Thelma and Tony met his eyes with questioning looks. 'She's putting the tools back. In about a couple of minutes she'll be starting. Hurry! There's not a second to be lost!'

Grabbing up the blankets between them, Thelma and Robert assisted Tony to his feet. They moved through the gap in the hedge and up to the garage. Standing well back among the shadows, they waited with bated breath.

The soft purr of an engine came to their ears. Then the garage doors were pushed open as they waited, tensed in every limb. There was another pause as Virginia returned to the car.

Further down the drive, the sergeant turned yet again in his sleep, and this time he awoke. He blinked and looked around him. How long had he been asleep? An uneasy feeling of guilt stole over him.

What was that sound? Surely it couldn't be a car, at this time of night? He listened again. It was — coming nearer, too!

He opened the door and stepped out onto the drive. Had he but taken one step further, it would have been his last; a large car swept past him, gathering speed as it went, and swung out into the open road. Turning his head in the direction whence the car had come, his eye fell upon three figures swiftly entering the garage.

Fumbling for his police whistle, he ran forward. But fate was against him, for those figures had spotted him also. One of the three detached himself from the others and ran down the path towards the sergeant, ostensibly with the friendly intent of meeting him halfway. When they drew level, however, before the befuddled policeman had time to raise his whistle to his lips, he received a crashing blow on the point of his jaw. He reeled backwards into the hedge, where he fell unconscious to the ground.

In the garage, Thelma and Tony, having set the engine going, were waiting for Robert's return. As he appeared in the doorway, Thelma moved over to make room for him. He jumped in, and as they started to back out, he turned round to Tony and pushed something into his hand.

'Your revolver,' he said. Tony took it eagerly.

Once on the drive, the car turned quickly; in went the gears, and they shot away towards the gate. As they passed the police car, Robert heard an explosion from the back; it was followed by another, even louder.

'The old police car,' Tony explained cheerfully. 'Thought I'd give it a parting shot. No use trying to be quiet now.'

As they turned at the end of the drive, Robert saw the wisdom of the remark, for he could just distinguish a figure at the head of the steps leading from the house. He turned the car into the open road, and fixing his eye upon a fast-disappearing tail-light in the distance, pressed his foot down on the accelerator.

The figure that had appeared so suddenly upon the steps was now running down the drive. When he reached the gate, he stopped; their car was almost completely lost to sight, and further pursuit was obviously impossible.

Muttering a few choice oaths beneath his breath, Detective Inspector Coleman stood, hands on hips, looking after them until the car became a mere light, and the light a speck, which speedily vanished altogether.

A voice by his side brought him round, to see his astonished assistant standing at his elbow. 'D'you see that?' his superior demanded wildly. 'The whole lot of them. Escaped from under our noses! I thought I told you to lock them all in, and check if they were all in their rooms before you did it?'

'Yes, Inspector. And I did!'

Detective Blake swallowed hard. This was the first time he'd ever seen the inspector in a rage, and he was tremendously impressed.

'Then they must have climbed out of the windows. I could have understood Harcourt doing it; he's got a reason for running away. But the others — it's beyond me!'

'D'you know how many of them have gone, sir?'

'I picked out three at least. And both cars have gone. It was the noise of the first one that brought *me* out.'

They both started gloomily retracing their steps back to the house.

'Got the numbers of those cars, have you?' the inspector inquired suddenly.

'Yes, sir.'

'Well, you'd better get on to the station and tell them to send out an SOS to all outlying stations between here and London. May pick them up that way, though they haven't located the doctor yet.'

'That's what I came out to tell you, sir. There's someone on the phone for you. Said something about Doctor Prescott — didn't quite catch it all, because that was when you started to shout, sir, and what with that and the car, and the, er, explosions — '

'The explosions? That's easily explained.'

They were now standing by the police car, the inspector gazing in a sort of morbid fascination at the punctured back tyre, which told them its own story.

'Why didn't you tell me about somebody being on the phone before?' he demanded sharply a few seconds later, when they had turned towards the house again.

'Well, sir, this other matter seemed so much more important at the moment — '

'Quite right. A damned sight more

important. I don't think the doctor's got anything to do with it. Stop!' He put a hand on the detective's shoulder and they both came to a standstill. 'Listen. There it is again.'

A low moan came from out of the shadows to their right. The inspector moved forward, and a few seconds later he was on his knees beside the prostrate body of Sergeant Ridgeway. Together they managed to raise him to a sitting posture.

'Is he badly hurt?' Blake inquired as the inspector made a brief examination of the sergeant's head.

'Yes,' came the reply. 'Nasty crack on the head. That'll be a lesson to him; teach him not to go to sleep on duty again.'

'But, Inspector, we don't know — '

'Of course we do,' he cut Blake short irritably. 'Come on! We'll carry him back to the house.' And between them, they carried him up the few remaining yards of the drive and into the hall. Once again the servants awaited them there, presenting an even more terror-stricken group than before.

Coleman had made up his mind to tell

them nothing, and in answer to Parker's ludicrous query of 'Anything wrong, sir?' he merely replied, 'Nothing, nothing,' and then 'Give us a hand with this chap into the lounge.'

As Parker stepped forward to help, so the other servants caught sight of the Sergeant. His face was streaked with blood and plastered with grime, while his hair was literally stiff with an ugly, sticky kind of matter that was fast congealing. They huddled together in a pale, terrified mass.

The inspector relinquished his hold of the sergeant to Parker, and after opening the door of the lounge for them to pass, returned to the study, where he slammed the door behind him and crossed hurriedly to the telephone. He was just replacing the receiver when Blake entered the room.

'He'll be all right,' he said without waiting to be asked, 'Parker seems to know quite a bit about first aid, so I've left him to it. Giving the servants the treat of their lives.'

'I wish they'd go to bed,' was the

inspector's gloomy comment. 'By the way, I've just rung up the station, so you needn't worry about that.'

'Oh, thank you, sir. Did you get your other message all right, sir?'

'No. They'd rung off; got tired of waiting, I suppose.' He rose wearily to his feet. 'And now,' he said with grim determination, 'we're going to go round to all those bedrooms and see what we can find. Come on!'

He had just opened the door when the telephone bell rang. Blake answered it. He turned to the Inspector. 'For you, sir.'

The inspector came and took the receiver from him. 'Inspector Coleman speaking . . . yes . . . what?' He looked over to Blake. 'Shut the door. It's that call I missed. Yes . . . I'm listening . . . Go ahead . . . '

15

The Open Road

Half an hour had passed, and every room had been searched. Down in the study, the detectives sat, both pale and anxious — and the mystery surrounding the death of Paul Conway seemed more impenetrable than ever.

The inspector broke the silence. 'Only a couple of hours ago, I was telling myself how easy it all was. I should have learnt at my age never to take things at their face value. Always deceptive — I was a fool.'

'I don't see that you're to blame, sir.'

'Don't you? Well, I am. When we first came down here, everything seemed so damned simple. I felt this case was going to bring us both promotion. Now it's going to bring us up on the mat; and it won't be for promotion either . . . ' And he relapsed into a moody silence.

Suddenly the inspector received one of

his more brilliant inspirations. 'Great Scott! Why on earth didn't I think of that before?' he cried.

Blake looked up sharply. 'Of what, sir?'

'Why Omar, of course — the fortune teller that Harcourt told me about!'

'But I thought you said, sir, that it was — '

'All boloney? I know I did; but we can all make mistakes, can't we?'

'Of course, sir. But how does that fit in with Harcourt's guilt?'

'It doesn't. But what I'm trying to say is, supposing he didn't do it after all? What then?'

'I don't know, sir. I haven't thought about it from that angle.'

'Better start now, then. Listen — our supposition that Harcourt was the murderer was sound enough, until all these other people made a bolt for it and blew the whole thing sky high. Five people have succeeded in leaving this house tonight — which argues all of them must know something they've been clever enough to keep from us. The only person who seems to have nothing up his sleeve so far is old

Fredericks, and he's slept through the whole thing, possibly out of sheer exhaustion.

'Now, if we assume that Harcourt's extraordinary story of hypnotic control has some grain of truth in it, then we have a motive for his leaving, do you see? He would obviously feel that the key to the whole mystery lay somewhere in that fortune teller's place in Bloomsbury, and decided to do a little private sleuthing on his own, in order to clear himself. That seems all fairly reasonable to me.'

Blake remained silent. Once things like hypnotism or telepathy or anything of that sort began to rear their ugly heads before him, all the materialist in him sprang into instant life.

'What are you frowning for?' the inspector barked at him irritably. 'Can't you believe it?'

'Frankly, no, sir.'

'Well, neither did I — at first. But hypnotism certainly exists, and telepathy might. And surely when a man gets to such a low state, and goes to pieces as Harcourt did, anything might happen to him, and — '

A discreet rap on the door cut short his

theorising. 'Come in,' he called.

The door opened, and Parker appeared on the threshold.

'How is he?' the inspector asked quickly.

'I've put him to bed, sir,' Parker explained. 'At the moment that's the best I can do. He came to about ten minutes ago, but went off again almost at once.'

'I see. Did he say anything?'

'He said it was Mr. Harcourt that hit him, sir.'

'Harcourt! It would be.'

'Will you be requiring me any further, sir?'

'No, thanks . . . Wait a minute, though. Do you know anything about cars?'

'A little, sir. I was a chauffeur for some years.'

'Good. Would you mind doing me a favour, or are you too tired?'

'I don't think so, sir. What is it?'

'The police car — out there at the end of the drive — one of the tyres has been badly punctured.'

'I see, sir. I'll do my best.'

'Thank you.'

If only he could put that car right — quickly! Quickly!

★   ★   ★

The rain was coming down in sheets as the storm returned. Visibility — except for the brief moments when the whole of the surrounding countryside was lit up by lurid flashes of light — became a matter of a few inches, headlights seemed almost superfluous, and car speed was cut down to barely thirty miles an hour.

Sitting behind the wheel, straining his eyes so as not to lose sight of the red tail-light ahead of him, Robert drove steadily forward into the remorseless torrent before him. During that dreadful drive, Thelma sat looking at him, her eyes glistening with admiration; she felt that her faith in him had been justified.

Then Tony finally put into words a suspicion that had been troubling him. 'Why aren't we being followed?' he demanded suddenly.

'I suppose because you ruined their car,' Robert said thoughtfully, careful not to take his eyes off the road.

'Oh, I didn't mean them,' came the bland reply. 'Don't the police get in touch with each other? You know, telephoning from station to station? That village we just passed — surely there was some sort of police station there? Why didn't they try to stop us?'

'Yes, Robert, why didn't they?' Thelma echoed. 'They must know all about us by this time.'

'I expect they do. But we didn't pass the station, that's all. Don't you remember, the sharp turn to the right we took halfway down the High Street? That was to avoid passing the police station. We made a half-circle round it and returned to the High Street about a quarter of a mile further on. I remember wondering what it meant at the time.'

'So that's what it was,' Thelma exclaimed in surprise.

'Virginia must know this part of the country pretty thoroughly. Probably she's clever enough to avoid every police station between here and London. If she is, she deserves a medal.'

'Rather!' Tony agreed from the back. 'Lucky we didn't run into a copper, though, wasn't it?'

Robert smiled. 'It was. I can't believe that she knows every policeman's beat around here as well; that'd be asking too much.'

The two men laughed together, but Thelma frowned. 'What makes you so sure we're going to London?' she asked.

'It's just intuition, that's all.'

'Based on some theory, maybe?' she inquired.

'It's much too complicated to tell you now,' Robert said. 'Later on, when I don't have to drive.'

They drove on in silence, each occupied with their own thoughts. But Fate had still many tricks left with which to torment them, and the next surprise was when the car took a sudden and unexpected turn to the right. Tony was the first to comment.

'Well, there goes your theory, Robert. It's goodbye to the London road.'

'I can't understand it' was all that he said, and in those few words he managed to convey all the agonising uncertainty he was feeling.

The thunder was now a distant muttering, and for the last ten minutes there had not been a single flash of lightning; by the end of the next half hour, the storm that had been so violent would have passed away altogether.

The rain was less heavy, and visibility had improved to such an extent that now not only could they distinguish the tail-light in front of them, but also the outline of the chassis, together with the number plate. It was these circumstances that roused Thelma from her state of melancholy. She leant forward intently and touched Robert on the arm.

'You can put your brakes on! That is not Virginia's car!' she said.

With a frenzied, defeated gesture, Robert jammed on his brakes; and with a loud jarring noise, followed by a wide skid along the wet surface of the road, they came to an abrupt standstill.

16

Great Minds . . .

When the last rumble of thunder had died away in the distance, the inspector was still seated at the desk, fuming with impatience; for so violent had been the downpour of rain that Parker, try as he would, had been forced to temporarily abandon his work on the car.

And it was only now, a good half hour later, that he was able to resume it. In the study the two men could hear his steps as he wearily trudged down the drive; wearily, not through unwillingness but from sheer physical exhaustion.

'If you don't mind my asking, sir, haven't we overlooked that telephone conversation you had a little while ago?'

'Telephone conversation?' The inspector looked at Blake, seated nearby.

'The one you had just before we made our search, sir.'

'Oh, that! Wasn't much help. It was just one of the men from the station at Uxbridge ringing up to say that they'd spotted the car YW7556 making for London.'

'Must have been the car we figured the doctor got away in, sir?'

'Suppose so. Thought I'd told you. Doesn't help much, but it backs up my theory about the key to this whole affair being in London — in Bloomsbury — in the black room.' The inspector rose impatiently to his feet. 'As soon as Parker out there can get that car fixed, I'm off to London. You can stay behind here and keep the red tape side of the thing going, while I get to the heart of it.'

By this time he had reached the window and was gazing out towards where the dark figure of Parker could dimly be discerned bending over the car. As he watched impatiently, Parker chose to straighten himself up. 'He's done it — he's done it!' Coleman pronounced excitedly, turning back into the room again.

And it certainly looked as though this were the case, for having straightened himself up, Parker was now running as fast as his legs would carry him towards the front door. A moment later, a loud rap announced that he was outside the study door.

'Come in!'

The door was thrown open, and Parker, quite unlike his normal self, dishevelled and breathless, hurled himself into the room. 'I saw a man — creeping up the drive, sir!' he gasped out.

'A man?' The inspector looked at him in amazement. 'Did he see you?'

'I don't think so, sir. He was on the opposite side to the car, creeping along by the hedge. It was only by chance I saw him. I happened to walk round the car to find something, and there he was; so I came straight in to tell you.'

'Quite right, too. You wait here. Blake, come with me.'

Leaving a harassed and nervous butler behind them, the two men hurried out of the room. *This'll take him off the car,* thought the inspector to himself as they made for the front door. For one moment, the idea of getting a car up from the nearest village presented itself to him, but he dismissed it at once. Up till now, the storm had made it almost impossible for any car to have come through to them, and now — well, the chap must have nearly finished the job.

The front door was open, and slackening their pace, they passed out onto the porch. The inspector turned to Blake by his side, and put his lips to his ear, whispering, 'Let's walk down to the car as though nothing's happened.' Blake nodded in reply.

They peered into the shadows on either side of them, but nothing could they see. Having reached the car, they found the punctured tyre and began examining it intently, thereby giving the impression it was to this end that Parker had fetched them from the house.

Still no sign of life. Parker's precipitate exit had evidently put the intruder upon his mettle; he would now be more cautious, and it might be some little time before he would be lured into disclosing his presence again. For the next few minutes this was obviously the case; then, quite suddenly, the inspector caught hold of Blake's arm. 'Look!' he hissed.

Blake obeyed, and sure enough the figure of a man could be clearly discerned moving along against the hedge on the opposite side of the drive. For a few minutes more they continued in their examination of the tyre; and then, when the figure had passed them, they walked behind the car as though to examine something at the back.

The moment they were beyond range of the intruder's eyesight, they darted across into the shadows; and keeping as close in to the hedge as he was, tiptoed after him.

They were soon within easy reach of him, and slowed down in order to give him the opportunity to make the next move. Now his footsteps grew slower and slower, while he made frequent stops. His attention was focused upon the house; that much was evident by the quick nervous glances he kept darting in that direction from time to time.

He paused when they were opposite the study. The sight of the lighted windows had forced their quarry to move more quickly, when the curtains were drawn back to disclose the nervous features of Parker looking out upon them. At the sight of his face, the man in front of them instantly shrunk even further back into the shadows, where he remained quite still.

'Damned fool,' the inspector thought to himself. 'As though he could hope to see anything on a night like this.'

Very soon, Parker dropped the curtains and removed himself from sight; and after a few minutes more the man began to move again. Now that their eyes were becoming accustomed to the darkness, they could see that he was of medium height, fairly thin, and according to what they could guess from his movements, no longer very young; these, and one other thing, they could tell even at this distance — he was wearing something over his head.

By this time they were nearing the porch, and the hopes of the two men ran high as they remembered they had left the front door open.

The man paused, moved back into the shadows again and ruminated.

The detectives moved carefully forward, until there was little space left between them.

Finally, the door proving too big a temptation for him, he slunk out of the shadows and crept across the drive. This gave the detectives their cue; and, stepping forward, they took him firmly by the shoulders. After a violent start, their prisoner made no further effort to escape, but walked quietly with them into the house.

Once inside, the inspector ripped off the scarf the intruder was wearing about his head, and turned him to the light. 'Good God!' he gasped as he caught sight of the man's face. For in that moment he received the greatest shock so far! As for Blake, he was speechless. And before he could gather his scattered wits, he received another even greater surprise; for the inspector, having discovered the man's identity, was now quite calmly winding the scarf round his head again as quickly as he could.

'Keep your face covered as much as possible,' he ordered in a low crisp tone. 'I don't want the butler to see you, or he'll never get that car done tonight.'

Without a word the man obeyed, restoring the scarf; and together the three of them entered the study.

Parker met them at the door. 'Have you got him, sir?' he enquired anxiously.

'Yes, thanks. Now you get along with that car.'

He sidled out of the room, casting curious glances at the muffled figure between them, but without daring to ask any further questions.

Immediately after he had gone, Blake shut the door, while the inspector conducted their captive to the chair facing his desk. 'Sit down,' he ordered sharply as he walked round and seated himself the other side, facing him. 'You can take that scarf off now.'

Obediently, the scarf was laid aside.

'And now,' said the inspector, leaning forward and looking him straight in the eyes, 'perhaps we shall be able to get somewhere.'

It was some time after the car had come to a standstill before any of them had the heart to speak. The first to break the silence was Robert, his voice bitter with disappointment:

'I suppose we lost her during that last downpour,' he muttered without looking up.

'I wonder if she knew she was being followed,' Thelma said. 'She must have heard the revolver shots, of course; but then, she mightn't have connected them with herself.'

'We kept as far behind as possible. Too far behind,' Robert added gloomily.

'What do we do now?' Tony asked, more seriously than was his wont.

'I suppose — we could go back to the manor house,' Robert suggested haltingly.

'After running away? Why, our position would be worse than ever,' Thelma protested.

'Of course it would,' Tony backed her up. 'They'd be down on us like a cartload of bricks.'

'They weren't too charming to us before, were they?' came Robert's hollow retort. 'But what else can we do?'

It was then that Thelma noticed a curious expression on Robert's face; one that could only have come upon him in the last few seconds. 'Robert,' she said gently, 'what are you thinking about?'

At first he did not answer. Then, quite suddenly — 'Just a moment, dear, and I'll tell you.' His voice had a certain vague quality about it, suggesting that his thoughts were far away from the immediate present.

As the two of them watched Robert intently, they saw an even stranger expression cross his face. For a little while that intense concentration continued — and then, without the slightest warning, it gave way to one of the most immense wonderment. He turned to Thelma and made as though to say something, but those words were never spoken, for at that moment the expression of wonderment vanished likewise, and its place was taken by that of distaste. After what appeared to be an intense mental struggle with himself, he spoke in a clear-cut, decisive manner such as neither of his listeners had expected.

'Thelma, if I told you I had a hunch, an intuition, have you sufficient faith in me to let me act upon it, and take you along as well?'

'Yes, of course, Robert.'

He leant back in his seat and looked searchingly into her deep blue eyes. 'Thanks, darling. You remember I had a hunch some time ago that Virginia was leading us to London? Well, I've just recalled something — something I'm afraid I can't tell you about just yet — but it fits in perfectly with that original theory of mine. Now, we can either go straight back to the manor house, admitting defeat, or else we take a chance on this whim of mine, and make for London. What's your answer?'

'The same as before, darling — London, of course.'

'I agree too,' Tony assented, 'though nobody seems to have asked me.'

A few minutes later, they were back on the London road. The storm had now completely cleared away, and the air was cool and fresh. Skiddy roads were the only danger, but otherwise everything was perfect. They kept up a steady sixty miles an hour, until on leaving the country roads they were obliged to reduce to the specified thirty.

As they slid through Uxbridge, Robert was smiling; perhaps this was why he drove so blatantly past the police station without giving it a second thought. Unfortunately for him, the police were not so careless — and within the next few minutes the information of their whereabouts was being telephoned to Inspector Coleman, who received it with great alacrity. Already he was preparing for his drive to London, and this new piece of information was therefore doubly welcome.

Little did Robert suspect as he drove on confidently through the darkness that another person, now miles away, had also this hunch concerning Number Nine, Queen's Court, Bloomsbury, and would all too soon be hot upon his heels.

They went on through Ealing . . . and

then came Marble Arch. Tony, who hadn't spoken a word for well over half an hour, considered it high time that he made an attempt to discover their destination. 'Do you feel at all inclined to tell us where you're taking us to, Robert?' he asked.

'Well, since you must know, we're going to Number Nine, Queen's Court, Bloomsbury — the salon of Omar, the fortune teller.'

'Well, I'm damned!'

'But Robert,' Thelma said incredulously, 'I don't understand. That was the place you went to before you — '

'Yes, dear. I can't explain now. But if I'm right, it won't be long now before you find it all out for yourself.'

She longed to ask him more; but before she had time to speak, Tony broke in upon her with a remark seemingly far removed from their present situation. 'Do you know much about the Joan Dycer case?' he asked her thoughtfully. 'You know, the woman who committed suicide?'

She looked at him as though he had suddenly taken leave of his senses. 'Why, yes,' she replied, trying to humour him, 'I know a little. We were discussing it tonight, don't you remember? But really I don't see — '

'What it has to do with the present? Oh, nothing much, except that this Omar chap was supposed to have been caught up in it in some way.'

'Really?' Although it had not been apparent to either of them, Robert had been listening intently the whole time. 'I don't remember any suspicion of the kind coming out in the papers. Your own theory, perhaps?'

'Partly. Rather an interesting one, though, don't you think? I must tell you more about it sometime.'

At that precise moment, they swept into Queen's Court. It was dimly lit and rather sinister, not a sound disturbing the stillness that surrounded it. Slowly the car advanced along the centre of the road. Halfway down, Robert switched off the engine and drew into the kerb. Without a word, he jumped out, and Thelma did likewise; then came Tony. There was no need to put into words the answer to their speechless queries — he merely pointed his finger. They followed it with their eyes, and all was suddenly clear.

Standing at the kerb a few yards up was a car spattered with mud as though from a long journey.

It was Virginia's car. Robert's hunch had come off!

17

The Black Room Again

As Virginia made good her escape from the manor house, she had no suspicion anything was amiss until she heard the shots as she turned onto the London road. Up to that moment, she was sure that she was alone. On hearing them, she accelerated immediately; and without daring to look round to see if she was being pursued, she shot blindly forward. Her mind was in a state of complete chaos, and when she finally took a hasty glance behind her and discovered that she was being followed, she became more confused than ever.

It never occurred to her that she was being followed by anybody other than the police; hence her careful avoidance of all police stations. Somehow or other they must have heard her starting up her car; but this did not account for the shots.

They obviously couldn't have been intended for her, because she was well out of the drive and some few yards down the road before they began. Then who could they have been meant for?

This question both puzzled and irritated her as she drove on. Then came the storm, and everything except the sheer act of driving was obliterated from her mind. Had it not been for this, she might have noticed sooner or later that it was not the police car that was pursuing her, but her sister's. Unaware of this, she battled on miserably through the storm and tempest of the night.

It was just as she was beginning to despair of ever shaking off her pursuers that the great chance came to her; and she saw, dimly through the curtain of rain, another car some little way ahead.

Taking her courage in both hands, she made a dash for it. In one wild spurt she had passed the car, and almost lost sight of it in the darkness behind her. She smiled to herself, scarcely daring to feel triumphant, for fear her little ruse should be discovered.

Thus she continued for some time, keeping her eyes unwaveringly upon the road and testing her driving skill to the uttermost. It was not until the storm had cleared away that she took the opportunity of looking round; when she saw a long empty road as far as the eye could reach. After this, she was not afraid to allow herself a moment's triumph.

Notwithstanding, she never grew careless, but continued in her method of avoiding police stations, and succeeded in reaching London without having passed a single one. It was not until she was nearing her destination that she began to ask herself for the first time if in undertaking this lone nocturnal drive she had done right.

Whatever was the outcome of this night's work, it looked like being extraordinarily unpleasant for her. However, she was not acting on intuition alone, she told herself, but on hard-won knowledge she had obtained only a few hours previously; and it was this and this alone that had made her present course of action so unavoidable.

As she turned into a deserted Queen's Court and beheld its long and ill-lit pavement and roadway, this feeling of trepidation came to her even more forcibly than before; and thus it was with an anxious feeling that she drew to a standstill outside Number Nine. After stopping, she sat quite still, endeavouring to think out her best plan of action. The effort of getting there alone had been so tremendous that it had left her no energy to think of anything else. But now the problem had to be faced.

She glanced up at the dark building she had gone to such lengths to reach. Grim and uninviting, all its windows darkened, desolate and heavy with grime, there seemed little hope of forcing an entry or of finding anything if one did. Indeed, at that moment, had it not been for her unwavering faith in herself and her powers of deduction, she would have turned back there and then.

At length she clambered slowly out of the car, taking with her a long, blunt instrument from among her tools. And gripping this firmly in her right hand

— after glancing quickly to either side of her — she crept hastily across the pavement and mounted the steps to the front door. While one hand firmly grasped the instrument, with the other she produced a torch from the pocket of her motoring coat and made a meticulous investigation of the front door. Realising the impossibility of forcing an entrance this way, she turned her attention to the windows. They all appeared to be heavily latched, and looked as though they had been so for many months.

Finally her attention was caught by a small window at the side of the door; this, as far as she could judge, was merely latched, with no other bolt or bar of any sort. Switching off her torch, she transferred it to her other hand and began to feel for something in her pocket. She soon found it; it was a penknife. She opened it, and carefully inserted the blade between the edge of the glass and the framework, pressing it slowly upwards. Soon she came up against something hard; she pushed and slowly it began to give. Putting down the instrument she had taken from the car on the window-sill, she pressed her other hand against the frame; gently she increased her pressure until the window noiselessly opened.

Hastily closing the penknife, she put it, together with the instrument, into one of her deep pockets; the torch she still grasped in her hand as she climbed into a kneeling posture upon the sill. Next she sat down, putting her hands out on either side; and bringing her legs round, she let herself down into the darkness, as a heavy curtain brushed against her face; and there she remained for a few seconds to compose herself before continuing.

She flashed on her torch again, being careful to keep the beam directed upon the ground; and she endeavoured to get some idea of the passage down which she was to travel. How long it was, she had no means of judging. Some way down she could spy a staircase, but it continued past this and was lost in the gloom beyond which her beam of light had no power to penetrate. The walls, she noted, were some neutral colour — possibly a dark grey — and the floor was covered in a thick carpet of the same shade. Also, there was no furniture of any kind as far as she could see. This much she learned before, having extinguished her torch, she crept forward.

Keeping well against the wall, she felt her way along; her feet sank into the heavy carpet, rendering her approach quite noiseless. She felt, as she had done on her previous visit, that same sinister atmosphere about the place.

She was just about to switch on her torch again, when she saw something: a light, very dim, far down the passage ahead of her. Her breathing quickened as she moved onwards.

At last she could see that it came from an open doorway right ahead of her. It must be the black room! She remembered now — it had been at the end of the passage. She crept to the side of the doorway and peeped in, her hands clenched themselves convulsively. Just as she'd thought!

Before her were the familiar black walls. The ceiling was lost in shadows, giving it the appearance of some lofty cathedral; though surely, from its sinister aspect, it must be dedicated rather to the worship of some satanic majesty than to that of any holy faith. Producing a small automatic, Virginia passed quietly through the doorway. From there she could see at the far end of the room another door, partly open. It was from beyond this door — from the inner sanctum — that the light originated.

Without wavering, she struck a course straight across the middle of the floor in the direction of this other door. So sure of herself was she, with the words she was about to utter ready upon her lips, that she increased her speed; and before she realised what had happened, she had crashed into something. Instantly the light overhead came on, and a voice, hard and terrible, came to her through the speaker at the end of the room.

'Another step and I shoot!' it hissed with deadly venom.

She obeyed and did not move. Looking down, she saw she was standing directly in the centre of the circle of light. The chair she had stumbled against lay on the floor at her feet. Automatically she bent to pick it up.

'Leave it where it is!' came the harsh command.

She obeyed as before, and stood looking about her. It was not long before she discovered a small aperture just below the speaker through which the vague outline of a revolver pointed at her. Of the face behind it, nothing was visible except for a misty silhouette.

She relaxed, and waited on in silence. Then the voice suddenly spoke again: 'Why have you come here?'

'To see you,' she replied carelessly.

'*What* are you?'

'I'm a journalist,' she answered curtly. 'You know that, too.'

'Was that why you kept coming here?'

'No.' She stood rigidly facing the revolver, and her voice was filled with a note of suppressed but burning anger. 'I'll tell you,' she said in a quietly dangerously tone. 'It's what I've been longing to do for some time. But before I do anything else, I should like to remind you of a sweet, innocent woman whom you ruined

— whose death, at her own hands, is upon your head. It's to revenge her that I've been coming here. Her name is — '

'Joan Dycer?' the voice cut her short, with a curious strangled cry.

'You remember her? Joan Dycer, a woman of twenty-two — young, pretty, happily married, with everything before her. Ruined by you and your soul-destroying organisation; her life turned into a living hell by your persistent threats, until broken and despairing, she threw herself into the river and took her secret with her to the grave. Her blood remains upon your hands, and nothing will ever wash them clean!'

'How do you know this?'

'She left a letter in which she told me all, and from that day I swore to drag you and your countless crimes into the light. That's what I intended to do, and nothing was going to stop me!'

'Nothing?' The voice had suddenly become crafty, the terror of a moment ago having completely vanished.

'Nothing — until this evening.' She bowed her head. 'I'm afraid I'm not strong enough to go through with it.'

'I see.' The voice was mocking.

'But although I may not be strong enough to be revenged upon you,' she added, raising her head, 'I will not tolerate the continuance of your crimes!'

'And what do you propose to do to prevent that? Go to the police?'

'Yes. If there's no other way.'

'Why have you not done so already?'

'Because I wanted to give you this one chance of getting away.'

'Very kind of you. And if I don't avail myself of this splendid opportunity, you go straight to the police. How simple! But supposing I prevent you from doing that? Suppose — only suppose — I were to kill you?'

'It would do you no good to kill me,' she said with complete calmness, 'because it's all written down, and would be in the hands of Tony Hargreaves directly my death was made known.'

'So you've thought of everything.' This time there was a touch of unwilling admiration in the voice. 'Tony Hargreaves,' it continued reflectively. 'I think, perhaps of the two of you, you are the more formidable! And now,' the voice continued suavely, 'since you have been so frank with me, I should like you to explain your reason for this intrusion tonight.'

'That's a totally different matter. It's to do with the murder of Paul Conway. I've a feeling you are the culprit!'

'Really? Aren't you letting your imagination run away with you, young lady? Upon what do you base this absurd theory?'

'Upon the fact that you're here tonight.'

'Is that all? Not much to go on, is it? Supposing I help you now? I'll give you a suggestion — what have you against the idea of my influencing *somebody else* to murder Paul Conway?'

'Robert Harcourt?'

'I'm not mentioning names; but isn't that far more plausible than to suppose I went to the trouble of doing it myself?'

'I don't know,' Virginia admitted in a troubled voice. 'But I do know that you had something to do with it!'

'And what motive could I have for wishing Conway dead?' The voice was quite calm now, giving the impression of a cat playing with a mouse.

'How should I guess that? I know so little about you when it comes down to it, although what I do know is quite foul and disgusting enough!'

The voice chuckled maliciously. The sight of this headstrong woman losing her temper was affording him the greatest pleasure. 'Again you are allowing your imagination to run away with you. Why should you suppose that the things you don't know about me are any worse than those you do? You are wrong; the things you have not discovered about me are my good qualities, which I have in common with every other human being, although you may find that hard to believe — '

'I do.'

'You have found me here under unfortunate circumstances. Your opinion of me has been falsely coloured by that stupid woman who — '

'Leave her name out of it, will you?'

'Just as you please,' the voice went on

in the same tone of smug satisfaction. 'Though you must admit that it is she who is to blame for all *this*. Had it not been for her committing suicide, rather than confessing to her young husband the illegitimacy of their child, all would still be well; and neither you nor I would be standing here tonight, facing one another.'

'Perhaps it's just as well that we are!' Her voice was proud, defiant.

'That, my dear child, remains to be seen.'

Those words brought home to her for the first time the true horror of her position. But not by the slightest quiver in her voice or facial expression did she betray the feeling of panic that had gripped her heart at that moment. 'You can't frighten me, Mr. Omar, so don't try.'

'I frightened you earlier this evening, if I remember rightly.'

'That was only because of the shock of seeing you — I wasn't prepared.'

'Are you prepared now?'

With a defiant toss of the head, she looked again towards the aperture behind which she knew her tormentor to be.

'Yes!' she replied.

'I'm glad to hear it. For whatever happens now, you can't accuse me of not being lenient with you. This evening I was prepared to spare you — to trust to your discretion. I thought you would be reasonable, and after you had recovered from your little shock, I counted on your silence. Until you appeared here a few minutes ago, your behaviour led me to believe that my judgment had been correct; but I was wrong. Not content with having received my warning, you must needs continue in this ridiculous escapade of yours, until you have become a menace to my peace — a danger — a woman in whose hands my very life may rest, in other words a woman who knows too much! There is only one way to deal with people like you — only one way to preserve my own safety, and that is the way I am going to take.'

Virginia opened her mouth to speak. A harsh, cracked voice quite unlike her own answered; and she listened, while the beads of cold perspiration stood out upon her trembling brow, as though to the words of another. 'What are you going to do with me?'

'I am going to kill you,' came the cool, ruthless answer. 'I shall shoot you — '

'*Look!*'

'*Virginia!*'

'*What's happened to her?*'

Three voices rang out from the open doorway. There was a concerted rush as Robert, Tony and Thelma raced across into the circle of light.

But all this was lost on Virginia, for before they were halfway across the room, she had sunk in a swoon to the floor.

Now they were all bending over her, when a voice of command brought them instantly to their feet. 'Put your hands up — all of you!' it barked at them through the speaker.

The three unwillingly raised their arms above their heads.

'Thank you, ladies and gentlemen,' the voice sneered back complacently.

Through the aperture below the speaker, Robert was the first to spot the blunt noses of two revolvers!

18

Trapped!

'A nice little party to be sure!' the voice declared cynically. 'And how did you all get in?'

'Through the window; somebody had left it open,' Robert spoke up fearlessly.

'All the windows in this establishment are locked every night. You must have forced an entrance.'

'Virginia must have opened it,' Tony whispered at his side. The man behind the speaker heard him nevertheless.

'Housebreakers too! Breaking into people's houses is a criminal offence! I should be acting within my rights if I sent for the police.'

'Don't make me laugh,' Robert replied contemptuously. 'Go ahead and try, that's all. We know enough about you — '

'To what?'

'To . . . Just try it, that's all!'

'I'm not at all sure that I won't,' the voice went on imperturbably. 'It might be a rather interesting experiment.'

A low moan drew all their attention back to Virginia. 'Thank God you're all here,' were her words as she opened her eyes and took in the whole scene for the first time.

'How much longer do we stay like this?' Tony burst out angrily, glaring into the shadows.

'So long as I choose,' came the calm reply. Then, to Virginia: 'Get up!'

Virginia rose unsteadily to her feet.

'Put your hands up! Now stand close to the others!'

She obeyed, swaying slightly against Tony in her efforts to keep herself erect.

'Now, get this straight: you're all four at a terrible disadvantage — I can see you but you can't see me. I have two revolvers here, and if any of you attempt to move I shall shoot — to kill! And it might interest you to know that I shall aim at neither of you two men, but at Miss Virginia Fredericks!'

'God! You swine — ' In his rage Tony

felt the violent words sticking in his throat.

Virginia turned to him, her usually calm bright eyes now clouded with terror. 'He means it too,' she whispered tremulously. 'He threatened to kill me just before you came in.'

'That'll do — I want to hear no more from you!'

'But it's true, you murderer! I'll tell them all — '

'Virginia darling, please!' Thelma's voice broke in upon her frenzied outburst, and Virginia fell silent.

Thelma, on the other hand, continued in a cold, almost impersonal voice: 'You're Mr. Omar, the fortune teller, I suppose?'

'I'm not here to answer questions,' came the reply.

Robert listened intently. Was it his imagination, or did the voice sound slightly less truculent?

'Then I take it that you are. In which case you can answer me one question: what motive had you for seeking to induce Mr. Harcourt here to murder my step-father? Tell me that!' she demanded.

They all four waited for the answer. When it came, it was couched in carefully ambiguous terms that formed a strange contrast to those of rough brutality that had preceded it.

'Is it on Mr. Harcourt's testimony alone that you are asking me this?' the voice questioned cunningly. 'Which I take it you believe implicitly?'

'It is, and I do.'

'In which case, I regret to inform you that it is a mere fabrication of lies.'

'Do you deny that I had an interview with you here this afternoon?' Robert broke in hotly. 'When you told me how I was to murder a man at midnight and what sign I was to know him by?'

'All lies. I have never seen you until now.'

'That's a lie!' Virginia declared. Robert and the others turned to her in surprise. 'I saw him coming out of here at five o'clock.'

'You did?' Robert said in amazement.

'Yes,' she went on, wildly. 'I was just going to ring the bell when you threw open the door and ran out.'

'I didn't see you.'

'Of course you didn't; you were too excited to see anybody.' She turned her attention once more in the direction of the speaker. 'And that was how I got in the first time,' she cried defiantly. 'As he came out, I ran in — so now you know.'

'Now I know,' the voice snapped out viciously. 'Quite a little crook, aren't you?'

'Quit the sarcasm,' Robert cut in. 'So was I here this afternoon or wasn't I?'

'I don't choose to answer that question. The subject is closed.'

'You even refuse to explain why you wished to have my step-father murdered?' asked Thelma in the same tone as before.

'The subject is closed.'

'Very well, then,' she said with a shrug of her shoulders. 'In that case, I shall continue to believe what I've been told.'

With which remark she turned to Virginia, who was eagerly inquiring of Robert how they had come to follow her. Robert explained as briefly as possible, including how he had knocked Tony out — a fact that seemed to Virginia to be quite inexplicable.

'I'd also seen you climbing down the drainpipe,' Tony explained to her. 'And knowing what a dangerous view the police would take of you trying to escape, I thought I'd try to stop you.'

Virginia shook her head in mock despair. Then she turned to the others again, as she remembered something. 'But even now, I don't see how you managed to get here,' she said, still puzzled, 'for I thought I'd given you the slip. How on earth did you get on my track again?'

'Robert had a hunch that the key to the whole mystery lay here; so, being in a pretty bad position already, we thought it was worth taking the chance on it — didn't we, Robert?'

But Robert did not answer Thelma, his mind being otherwise occupied. He'd just realised that throughout the past few minutes they had not once been disturbed by the voice from the speaker. The revolvers still pointed at them, it was true; but something told Robert that the hands that should have been holding them were employed elsewhere.

'Ssh!' He put his finger to his lips; he would test this theory. He took a step forward and waited. Nothing happened. He took another and waited again; still nothing happened. He prepared to take a third —

'Get back to your place!'

He turned and walked back to the others; he was feeling vaguely puzzled, although his faith in his theory had not completely vanished by any means.

'Because I've let you lower your hands, it doesn't mean I'm asleep.'

Robert looked round, realising that they must have all lowered their hands automatically without thinking. 'We thought something had happened to you,' he retaliated sarcastically. 'You can't expect to keep us here forever, you know.'

'When do the police arrive?' Tony asked.

'That'll do. How many of you have got weapons?'

Nobody answered.

The voice grew impatient. 'I'm not in the habit of allowing people to fool with me,' it said in harsh tones. 'You'll all throw your weapons upon the floor;

otherwise, it would be a pity to shoot Miss Fredericks!'

Robert, Tony and Virginia threw their revolvers to the ground.

'Thank you, ladies and gentlemen.'

Robert again fixed his eyes on the space below the speaker; this time he could definitely distinguish a hand holding each of the revolvers, together with something that glittered fitfully in the darkness. The moment those hands were withdrawn, it would be the signal for action; and withdrawn they must be, of that he was convinced. The revolvers were left, supported by something or other, whilst their captor carried on with his task of cleaning up whatever incriminating evidence there might be in that room beyond. That was why he was playing for time, so as to finish what he had come to do. Robert smiled grimly to himself as he saw the situation clearly before him. If nothing was done, Omar, along with his alibi, would vanish completely into the blue; and it was he and he alone who could prevent this catastrophe from coming to pass.

He waited, never letting his eyes wander for an instant from the aperture. And so they remained, until Tony burst out with the obvious question that Robert had been so careful to avoid: 'Why are you playing for time?' he demanded angrily of the man behind the speaker.

Before any answer came, Virginia suddenly burst out again, even more violently than before: 'I know why he's playing for time — I've known it all along, ever since you all came into this room! He's keeping us all here because there's someone he knows he'll — '

But she never finished what she was going to say. For a shot rang out, as Tony, with incredible swiftness, jumped in front of her. Her sentence ended in a horrified gasp while Tony grasped his arm with an exclamation of agony.

'Are you hurt?' Robert asked anxiously.

'Not much. I'm all right,' Tony gasped, wincing. 'It got me in the arm, that's all!

'The price of chivalry, my dear Mr. Hargreaves,' the voice jeered at him.

'We'd better bandage it for him,' Robert said.

'I'll do it,' volunteered Virginia, now white as a sheet. 'Will you sit on the ground, dear? Then I can get at it better.' This sudden occurrence seemed to have transformed her back to her normal, level-headed self, who had battled her way through life unaided until now, and was prepared to go on doing so, come what may. With several of their hand-kerchiefs tied together, she managed to improvise a pretty workmanlike bandage, and to staunch in some small degree the stream of blood that was running freely from an ugly jagged wound above the elbow.

As Tony lay there, pale but determined to make light of his injury, Robert could not help feeling a great wave of admiration for him. It only went to prove how mistaken one's judgment of a man could be. But then, there was some mystery about him — something as yet none of them, with the possible exception of Virginia, knew anything about. 'You know that was a damned plucky thing you did just now,' he said warmly.

Virginia looked up at him. 'One has to

be brave in a job like his,' she declared.

'What *is* Mr. Hargreaves's job, we should be interested to know?' the voice inquired in its silkiest tones.

'Oh, Tony, I'm so sorry. I didn't mean to — ' Virginia began.

'It doesn't matter now,' he said. Then he looked past her at the speaker. 'My job — since you're so interested to know — is chief crime reporter for the *Daily Sun*. And as it is my speciality to report on crimes, I've been keeping my eyes on you for the past few weeks, Mr. — Omar!'

The significant pause before the name 'Omar' did not pass by Robert unnoticed.

'Really?' the voice continued as smoothly as ever. 'And what have you discovered about me, Mr. Hargreaves?'

Tony glared at the speaker aggressively. 'I know all about the Joan Dycer case, together with several others. And I know all about your business too, if you can call it that. So I made up my mind that I'd help Virginia to unmask you, if it took the last drop of my blood.'

'Very courageous of you, my friend. And is that all you know?'

This last question was framed in such a crafty way that Tony instinctively felt he had already said too much. 'It's all I'm telling you for the moment,' he concluded abruptly.

'But I don't understand,' Thelma said, frowning. 'What's this Joan Dycer woman got to do with it, anyway? I remember you mentioned her before.'

'She just happened to be one of his victims, that's all,' Tony explained. 'Only, she also happened to be a friend of Virginia's — that's why I'm more interested in her than the others.'

'But what is he guilty of?' Thelma asked. 'Is he a fake?'

'No such luck,' Tony replied bitterly. 'I wish to God he were! He happens to be about the finest hypnotist in the country. That's the danger of him. He's so good, he can get people's most intimate secrets out of them without giving them the slightest inkling of what's happening. That's what he did in the case of Joan Dycer: found out the one and only precious secret in her life, and then — well, his demands became so exorbitant that one morning the river police found her body washed up by the tide. And she was only one of them!'

'How dreadful!' Thelma's eyes flashed with fury.

'You've said it! His must be one of the biggest blackmailing rackets in history.'

'You flatter me, Mr. Hargreaves; I couldn't have explained it better myself.'

'You're going to pay for it, though, if it's the last thing I do.'

'It possibly will be if you're not very careful. I perceive you're not nearly so sensible about this matter as I at first imagined.'

'You were at the end of your tether without my interference — you wouldn't have got away with it much longer, anyhow.'

'That we unfortunately have no opportunity of seeing. I concur, however, your use of the word 'interference'. Interference — which shall cease, from this moment!'

'There's one thing I should like to ask you, though,' Robert cut in, addressing himself to Tony. 'Why your disguise?'

'Do you suppose if I went around looking all bright and alert, criminals, or even prospective criminals, would ever give away any of their plans in front of me? They'd be too much on their guard. It's when they think you're of no account that they'll begin to talk — particularly if you're always falling asleep. I've heard more confessions while pretending to be asleep than at any other time in my career.'

Robert smiled. 'Good for you!' But a quite different question rose to his lips, which he had great difficulty in restraining. For it was suddenly borne in upon him that Tony had possibly the same theory concerning the murder of Paul Conway as himself. It needed a great deal of will-power to keep back that question, and to be content to let events take their course.

Once again, Robert stood gazing at the aperture for several moments before taking the evidence of his own eyes. For the second time that night, he had seen the revolvers pointing at them with no hands visible behind them! 'Virginia,' he said in a whisper, 'give me your torch.'

She took it out of her pocket and handed it to him without a word. He took it and held it behind his back; then he cast another glance below the speaker. Assured that all was well, he bent down and retrieved the three revolvers. He handed one to Virginia, and another to Tony. They accepted them in silence, slipping them into their pockets. Then, holding his own revolver and the torch behind his back in both hands, he gave his final instructions.

'I expect you've guessed by this time that we're not being watched — that's why I'm going to take a risk. Tony, are you strong enough to stand?'

'You bet I am!'

'Good. Well, I'm going to shoot the lights; it's our only chance. When I do that, there's bound to be a bit of a firework display, so I want you to see that both the women keep well out of the way — against the walls. I expect you to be responsible for them.'

'And what are you going to do?'

'I'm going to try and get through that door in the wall — I think I can find it.

You possibly remembered it was open when we all came in?'

'So it was!'

They all remembered, although, like himself, none of them had seen it close. 'Now, Tony, see if you can stand.'

It was not as easy as he had anticipated — he had lost a lot of blood, and the bandage was slowly turning red as more soaked through it. But he made it to his feet. Pale as a ghost, he leant against Virginia, a faint smile playing about his lips.

'Right,' Robert continued, 'be ready then, all of you!'

At that moment they were arrested by the voice again; this time it seemed a little more emotional, as though its owner were labouring under some sort of strain — although the first words sounded commonplace enough. 'Standing, Mr. Hargreaves?' it purred solicitously. 'Not so badly wounded, after all?'

'None of your fault that I wasn't!'

'You've only yourself to blame for that. And now, I will tell you something,' the voice said. 'I have made up my mind what

I intend to do with you all. I wish you all to raise your arms again!'

Everybody obeyed, including Tony.

'I'm very sorry to cause you all this inconvenience — particularly Mr. Hargreaves,' the voice went on. 'But I'm afraid it's unavoidable. You see, it will not be for very long — you will soon know, all of you, what is about to happen, and then your discomfort will be at an end without the formality of an explanation being necessary.'

Robert's voice rang out suddenly. 'I thought so! Mr. Omar, you don't have to explain anything — because we know already! We know you've been preparing your getaway for the last ten minutes,' he carried on remorselessly. 'And we know also that you're counting on us being sufficiently green to stand here doing nothing while you get on to that fire escape at the back. I noticed it when we came here. Well, see that you don't underrate your opponent, Mr. Omar — because we're not quite so blasted simple as you think! And just by way of proving it to you . . . '

A shot rang out, followed by an explosion as the room was plunged into darkness.

Another shot rang out almost simultaneously, as Robert instinctively sidestepped. It was well for him that he did!

Tony had pulled the two women over towards the wall, where they cowered together in silence.

Then, to their great surprise, a beam of light cut across the room from Robert's torch, and for a fleeting second fixed itself upon the aperture.

That second, however, told him what he wanted to know. The tell-tale glitter he'd noticed earlier on had given him all the evidence he needed, and once again the room was swallowed up in the darkness; out of which his voice — firm and clear — hurled its challenge fearlessly: 'I shouldn't wear that ring if I were you, Mr. Fredericks!' he cried aloud.

A shriek of rage filled the air — two revolver shots, answering one another; then a silence; and finally a rending crash as Robert, having found the door, hurled himself against it with all his might!

19

Design for Killing!

The lock gave way, and Robert staggered into the room beyond. Recovering his balance, he looked around him. He saw the figure of a man in the middle of the room, writhing in agony as he vainly strove to staunch the blood that gushed forth from a wound in his hand. Robert's single shot in the dark had taken effect.

A curt command brought the man's hands above his head, and Benjamin Fredericks, shaking and white as death, prepared to confront his accusers.

While the two men faced one another thus in silence, the women and Tony stole into the room. Virginia was the first of the little party to enter, and she showed no surprise at all at the identity of their ex-captor. Next came Tony, who likewise showed the utmost unconcern. But Thelma acted quite differently; all the horror and misery that

320

were within her coming out in her one startled cry: '*Father!*'

The effect her appearance had on Benjamin was no less sensational. He became paler than ever, and her cry seemed to have acted like a sharp sword plunged into his heart. He closed his eyes while his whole body sagged under the strain. For a moment he looked as though he might collapse altogether.

'Here, sit down.' Robert pointed to the chair behind him, and Benjamin slumped into it, hiding his injured hand behind him.

Thelma remained silent, continuing to gaze at him, as though still scarcely able to credit the evidence of her senses.

Virginia helped Tony to a chair, while Robert, still keeping his revolver levelled at Benjamin, moved further towards the centre of the room. Without taking his eyes off his charge for more than a few seconds, he looked about him.

The room was about half the size of the one they had just left. It was decorated in black, and the only light came from a small reading lamp on the writing-desk;

this and one or two chairs completed the furnishings. From the wall that divided the two rooms protruded the back of the speaker, below which hung a microphone; and there was also a sliding panel, still open, through which the revolvers pointed, resting inside their cunningly concealed niches in the framework.

He cast his eyes behind the prostrate man sitting in the chair towards the fireplace and again he saw what he had expected; in the grate was a heap of ashes. Possibly they had been testaments of his many crimes, but Robert could not help feeling glad in the knowledge that at least some of his deeds could be commuted to the past and buried decently far beyond the ever-searching fingers of the law. The only other feature of the room was a large window, exactly opposite the microphone, which was wide open, disclosing in the uncertain light of dawn the iron steps of a fire escape.

Benjamin's voice — now suddenly grown weak and tired — brought Robert back from these speculations to the grim realities of the present. 'Why have you done this to me?' The remark was addressed to Virginia.

'I haven't done anything to you,' she answered calmly. 'I merely followed you here to try and reason with you.'

'How did you know I'd come here? You didn't see me leave?'

'Somebody else did, though — Doctor Prescott. That was why he disappeared.'

'Doctor Prescott disappeared?' Benjamin exclaimed.

'Yes. Soon after you, I expect. It was when I heard the police looking for him that I conceived the idea of slipping through the communicating door to see if you were still in the house.' Her voice sounded as unruffled as ever.

Robert broke in excitedly: 'But why should the fact that the doctor had gone make you think your father had done the same?'

'Because I knew the doctor well enough to realise that he'd never run away from anything to shield himself. Therefore, it followed he must be doing it for a friend; and the only friend of his at the manor house last night was Father.

When I'd passed through the communicating door,' Virginia continued, 'the first thing I did was to go over to the bed and see whether Father was there or not.'

'And he wasn't,' Robert concluded for her, now thoroughly caught up in the excitement of the moment.

'No. But somebody else was. Saunders!'

'You mean the fellow who works here?'

'I do. Saunders had been carefully planted there so as to disarm any suspicion should the police take it into their heads to enter the room before Father's return.'

'Where is he now?' The query came from Benjamin, concerned for his colleague.

'Still in your bed, I expect,' came his daughter's scornful reply. 'When I entered the room, he was lying with his back towards me; and though I was near enough to catch a glimpse of his face, I managed to slip back into my own room without his seeing me.'

'But I don't understand,' said Tony, forgetting for the moment the pain in his shoulder. 'How did he get down there? How did he come to be on the spot, just when he was wanted?'

Virginia smiled sardonically. 'He didn't have to get down there,' she explained. 'He *was* there. For the past few weeks he's been coming down regularly at weekends as a jobbing gardener and living in a little hut in the grounds.'

'Good God!'

'I suppose after Father granted me my first interview down here, just to find out what I was after, he thought things we're getting a little hot, so he asked Saunders to keep near at hand in case of emergencies. Still, it was a pretty good disguise all the same — I'd seen him once or twice in the distance, but even then I didn't recognise him until tonight.'

Robert looked at her in amazement. 'Saunders as a gardener,' he murmured dazedly. 'Well, I'm damned!'

'Saunders was a highly efficient man,' Benjamin cut in with a voice of ice. 'Failing to notice Virginia was the first mistake he's ever made.'

'Not the first, Father,' she reminded him, her eyes meeting his daringly. 'The second. He made his first this afternoon, when he shot at that beautiful crystal of yours — the crystal in which I saw your reflection as you came out of this very room!'

'So that was why you behaved so strangely tonight,' Tony murmured quietly. 'And that was what you were going to tell me at midnight in the lounge.'

'I should never have told you, Tony,' she said, shaking her head. 'Never as long as I lived, if we hadn't all come here tonight. That was why I let you come out of your room and go down to the lounge while I was standing with Robert and Thelma, watching you all the time.'

'But couldn't you trust me with it, darling?'

'It wasn't a question of trusting anybody. I'd come down to speak to Father — to tell him that I would be a party to his secret.'

'Virginia!' Benjamin looked up in surprise.

'And after telling him, I was coming down to you to beg you to drop the Joan Dycer case. That, although my father thinks I feel nothing but hate towards him, was what I intended to do!' She looked away from her father and put an arm round Tony, who gazed at her with a slight affectionate smile, before speaking.

'You needn't have troubled about keeping it from me,' he said. 'You see, dear, I knew it all the time.'

She looked at him in amazement.

'Yes. You see, in order to get a line on the Joan Dycer case, I used to come here in the early evening, just about the time when Omar was supposed to close for the night — and wait outside to see him coming out. On three of those occasions I saw your father.'

'But why didn't you tell me?'

'Because at first I took him to be a client. A brief talk with him down at the manor house, however, soon disposed of that theory. It was then, in order to be certain of my facts, that I commenced trying to discover a few more things on my own.'

'Did you succeed?'

'Not until tonight. But the fact that I was trying to do so must help you to understand my boorish behaviour before your father and your guests.'

Virginia turned towards Robert. 'I came here tonight because I knew instinctively that it was where my father would be; but what reason you could have had for coming here, I've yet to learn.'

'It wasn't a reason, but an instinct, much the same as yours,' Robert confessed in slow, measured tones. 'Something I remembered, just after we'd lost you in the storm, which made up my mind for me finally. Until then, I'd been all in favour of returning to the manor house and giving ourselves up.'

'After you'd lost me in the storm, Robert? But I don't understand; it doesn't make sense.'

'Oh yes it does,' he replied grimly. 'What I remembered in those helpless, despairing moments after losing you proved conclusively that a real link existed between the weird happenings at the manor house and this place in Bloomsbury. I remembered who it was that first induced me to pay my visit to Omar!'

'But didn't you know before?' Tony asked.

'I was tricked into going — put into a hypnotic trance — by you!' He pointed at Benjamin, who dropped his head before his accusing eyes.

'It was my last visit — when I was weak and half tight, and you took me into your study where you put the idea into my head of visiting Omar. It was too delicate a job to undertake in the surroundings of your home, I suppose, so you made me come here.'

'That's what you meant when you told the doctor he'd fainted once before!' Virginia cried, looking at her father as the thing began to take shape before her.

Benjamin raised his head and returned their glances fearlessly. Obviously nothing could be gained by prevaricating now.

'And God help me, I was fool enough to fall for it all,' Robert broke in bitterly. 'Why, you even found time enough to force me to write out the address and put it into my pocket so as to avoid any mistake. But you failed in one thing — thank God! You couldn't make me forget!'

'No. Had I been able to do that, all

might still have been well with me — had I not also made the mistake of forgetting to remove this tell-tale object.' He looked down at his hand, upon the second finger of which the ring still sparkled.

Robert nodded. 'That was the final proof!'

The moment he had uttered these words Tony, now impatient to get at the root of things, addressing himself to Benjamin. 'Now I think it's your turn to do a bit of explaining,' he growled. 'Tell us what all this means.'

'I should have thought you knew that already,' Benjamin said with a smirk.

'Well, we don't. There's no point in refusing now, because if you do we shall just go straight to the police; and they might not be quite so considerate as us.'

'Perhaps not. But what would you tell them, my friend? About my — blackmailing transactions, as you term them? All the substantial proof you might have had lies in that grate — charred pieces of paper, ashes, whose tale will never be told.' He glanced towards the fireplace with insufferable satisfaction. 'As to my other activities, what can you say of them? What have you to go upon, except the wild story of our friend Harcourt here, who tells you how I sought to persuade him to murder myself? Slender stuff, ladies and gentlemen! Go to the police and see how much importance they will attach to it.'

'How about the way you've treated us tonight?' Robert asked aggressively, determined not to be defeated by such glib reasoning. 'How about your threats to murder Virginia?'

'Tell them and see what they think of it! Is it not possible they might take a story of that sort as a fabrication of lies designed to cover up your own reasons for breaking into my house in the early hours of the morning? Remember that none of you have any right to be here; that you're all housebreakers! Go ahead and see how they will credit you!'

They looked at one another in dismay.

'Father! Will you explain your part in all this — if I ask you to?' Thelma spoke for the first time since they had entered.

The triumphant smile faded from

Benjamin's face; a fleeting expression of wild, agonising despair crossed his features, like a swiftly passing cloud. When he spoke, it was in the manner of one who is lost, and damned beyond redemption. 'Very well, then; I'll tell you.'

Instinctively they all drew nearer, but before he could begin, his face had blanched with pain, as with a great effort he drew his mutilated hand from behind him and laid it upon his knee.

'Your hand!' Thelma cried, and ran to his side.

'I hurt it — in the dark,' he explained carefully.

'Let me tie it up for you.'

He pointed towards the desk. 'You'll find a first-aid box in there.'

As she obeyed and went to the desk, Robert cursed himself inwardly for not having attended to her father's injuries before. He'd been completely carried away by the exciting events.

Having found some bandages, Thelma came back to Benjamin's side and fell upon her knees. Just as she was preparing to gently lift up his hand, however, he spoke, and in tones so filled with agony that it tore her heart to hear them.

'Thelma, darling,' he said quietly, 'before you do this, I should like to tell you something ... If you bandage my hand, you are doing so to the hand that murdered Paul Conway!'

Silence, deep and impenetrable, followed this outspoken confession.

Dismay clouding her beautiful eyes, Thelma took his wounded hand in hers and methodically began bandaging it.

'Do you wish to hear any more?' he inquired in the same dead voice.

'All!'

Turning his head towards the woman by his side, Benjamin took a deep breath. 'In order to give you a clear conception of how the tragic events of this night have come about, it is necessary to go back several years, to the time when Thelma's mother died,' he began.

'With Helen I spent the only really happy years of my life. She brought out all that was best in me; unlike my first wife who, through no fault of her own, seemed only to bring to the surface all that was worst in me. It was my treatment of her that caused the rift between myself and my brother Isador: he having been in love with her himself for many years before I married her.

'When my second wife died, therefore, my whole world crumbled about my ears, like so much dust. There was nothing left to live for — the whole meaning of life seemed to have been suddenly and brutally wrenched away. I was middle-aged by then, and set in my ways, so it was improbable that I should ever fall in love again, even had the thought of doing so been tolerable to me, which it was not. And yet, I had become so dependent upon Helen for even the smallest amenities of life that the thought of struggling on alone horrified me, and made the future appear as dismal and sombre as had been the past before I met her.

'It was then, when I seemed over-whelmed with my grief, that I noticed more strongly than before the striking likeness between my wife who had died and the daughter she had left behind her to brighten my declining years. From that time onwards, Thelma became all my care. I had always loved her, better far than my own daughter, God forgive me — but now she became the whole substance of my life.

'For some time all went well. Thelma reciprocated my affection as warmly and spontaneously as I gave it her, and life became nearly as pleasant and contented as it had been before — with one exception. Coming out of a restaurant in London one day, I happened to run across an old associate of mine whom I had not seen for many years . . . Saunders. He and I had run establishments such as this one we're in now, in practically every capital of Europe, at some time or another, and had made, by these same means I have been employing here, a vast amount of money. My share in the profits I had saved and invested successfully, so that when I married Helen I took a vow never to return to such activities again. Saunders, on the other hand, had spent unwisely, gambled and drunk the greater part of his share away, and at the time of our meeting was practically down to his last farthing. What more natural then, on his part, than to suggest a renewal of our former partnership?

'I refused at first; then weakened and prevaricated; but finally I agreed — with the result that we started a modest establishment at a house in Maida Vale. To begin with, I was fearful my powers should have deserted me; but I need not have worried, for everything worked out as smoothly as it had done before. It was only a matter of a few months before we were well on the path to success. Which path, needless to say, led us here.

'To all of you, blackmail obviously seems a terrible thing. To me, however — although I can appreciate in some small degree the sufferings of its victims — it appears as reasonable as any other mode of living whereby one battens upon the mistakes of others; so we will leave it at that. Anyway, it comprises the least important part of my story, for the portion that more intimately concerns all of us here tonight is that which is connected with my home life at the manor house.

'And this now suddenly experienced an entirely unlooked-for emotional upheaval. For Thelma had fallen in love with Robert Harcourt! The news, when it was first told to me by Thelma herself, filled me with dismay. Why I had not foreseen that sooner or later it would almost inevitably happen, I cannot think. Thus, coming as it did, the shock took me completely off my guard; and the picture of lonely, miserable desolation I imagined I had put behind me forever returned once again to torment me.

'I waited. I met Robert. I made myself as pleasant as possible and watched with agonised intensity the growth of their passion. Could it be a passing infatuation? I asked myself. But the months slipped past, and seemed to contradict any such supposition.

'Then, about five months ago, I began to detect a change in their relationship — a certain tension that had not existed before. And on questioning Thelma upon this unhappy state of affairs, I was told that Robert had fallen in with a bad set of people; he was drinking more than was good for him, and at the same time recklessly squandering his money.

'I was sympathetic with her, never daring to suggest that she should give him up. But I had seen a gleam of hope! And throughout the days and nights that followed, it strengthened as I perceived the rift between them growing wider with each successive meeting.

'It was not long, however, before another person appeared upon the scene — one who was far more difficult to deal with than ever Robert could have been. I refer — as you all have doubtless guessed — to Mr. Paul Conway. He, as you know, was the head of a private detective agency, an organisation that was nearly as illegal as my own. For the saying that no criminal need face the judge had he but enough money to make peace with Conway's Detective Agency, was, as what I am about to say will prove, nothing short of the truth.

'To be brief, one of Paul Conway's clients was a woman who had . . . suffered, I suppose is the correct term, through me; and Paul, sensing something unusual about the case, undertook to solve it himself.

'Whatever we may think about him personally, and I had greater cause to hate him than any of you, Paul was a very clever young man. So clever was he that in less than a month he had cut his way right into the core of my business — a thing the police in practically every corner of the world had failed to do before him. Naturally I had no choice but to make my peace with him in hard, cold cash. Which I did. And being filled with a certain unwilling admiration for him, we struck up what must have been one of the strangest friendships that have ever existed.

'The climax of this was reached when, barely more than six weeks ago, I was imprudent enough to invite him down to the manor house to spend the weekend with us. There he met Thelma; and whether from lust or love — we shall never know which — declared that nothing short of marriage with her would persuade him to hold his peace concerning my activities in London.

'Now I was in a cleft stick indeed, and could see no way to turn. The only possible escape from him was to marry her to Robert, and that idea was worse than death to me. As it was, Thelma chose this moment to break off her engagement with Robert, thereby robbing me of any vestige of an excuse with which to hold Paul at bay. At every meeting he grew more insistent, until at length I realised that there was no possible method left whereby I could longer avoid pressing his suit with her.

'This I set about; and loving me as she did, she consented, thinking all the while that she was pleasing me by doing so. Having been driven thus far, I solaced myself with thoughts of divorce and even half-convinced myself that could I but make their engagement long enough, he would eventually get tired and press for marriage no further. And then, if all else failed, I could always comfort myself in the belief that I and I alone was the only person whom she really loved.

'But it was not long before even this was denied me. For although she did not love Paul, it soon became evident in her every word and gesture that despite the fact she had broken from him, her heart was still given irrevocably to Robert. This thought maddened me beyond all bounds, and I was determined to break her love for him if it was the last and only thing I did! But, as is always the case, all this was easier said than done; and it took me a long time and a great deal of thought before I hit upon the plan I put into operation tonight.

'I knew that tales of his dissipation would do little to shake her love for him — it needed something far more subtle and original; and my plan seemed to be both. Her strongest characteristic, apart from her love for Robert, was her affection for me. What, then, if she should witness with her own eyes an attempt on the part of the man she loved to take the life of the man whom she had grown to regard as a father? This would surely convert her love to hate, and smash once and for all any possibility of an alliance with Robert. And without more ado, I put it into practice.

'How I did this, Robert can tell you better than I, since my power to make him forget the trances I put him into appears to have failed so lamentably. The rest of the plan was elementary. Robert was to come to my room at midnight with the intention of murdering me, the thought having been previously planted in his brain earlier in the evening. Thelma would see him, cry out maybe, and all would be over.

'Having had him so completely under my control already, it would require only a second to bring him as suddenly out of his trance as he had been put into it. Besides which, one can never induce a person to actually commit a murder unless the desire to kill be buried somewhere deep down in the subconscious mind, waiting but for this occasion to reveal itself. In Robert's case, I felt pretty safe in supposing that this desire was absent; in consequence of which, although he might go so far as to put his hands around my throat, nothing could force him to exert the pressure with which to take my life. This assumption I still believe would have proved correct, had not fate taken a hand in the proceedings before that point was reached, and so prevented me from witnessing the physical proof thereof.

'Fate took a hand in the shape of Mr. Paul Conway. All was going well; I'd arranged for Thelma to come to my room, Robert was downstairs merely waiting for the clock to strike the hour of midnight, and as I returned along the corridor I was filled with exultation and pleasure as I thought of the triumph so nearly within my grasp.

'Imagine my horror when on crossing the threshold I came face to face with Paul, an insolent smile playing about his lips, as he lay stretched out upon my bed. In that instant I went stone cold from head to foot, as automatically I closed the door behind me and came across the room to him, demanding what it was he wanted of me.

'On seeing the expression on my face, his smile broadened, while he drawled in blasé tones some insulting comments concerning his bedroom, concluding with the announcement of his intention to spend the remainder of the night in my room, while I, in my position as host, betook myself to his, where I should have ample opportunity to decide for myself whether all the things he'd said about it were true or otherwise.

'I replied, as civilly as I knew how, that this was impossible, and besought him to go. But he merely shook his head — and the hands of my watch moved nearer and nearer to midnight! Suddenly his tone changed; so did the subject of his conversation, and he began upbraiding me with my lack of enthusiasm in the announcing of his engagement.

'On and on he went until I felt I should go mad. Now he was talking of marriage — marriage! God, how could I ever allow her to marry such a man as that? Then — he made some obscene joke about her, and I realised why he had been so anxious to change his room. ' 'I know you think it sounds disgusting,' he cried as he saw my face turn pale with anger, 'but you can't call it rape nowadays because the women are all too eager. Why, I tell you — '

'And there he stopped, for he could see

me slowly advancing upon him. Not a sound did I make; only by the expression of my eyes could he divine the murderous intent that was within my heart. He seemed fascinated; the smile faded from his face and a look of stark terror took its place. But not one word did he utter, for he was paralysed with fright.

'As my hands seized him roughly by the throat, he gave a hollow gasp; that was all. I tightened my pressure until his face went black, his discoloured lips fell apart, his tongue lolled heavily out from between them — then, and not till then did I let him go. For my rage was appeased! As his lifeless body fell back upon the bedclothes, I found myself, to my great surprise, as cool and unruffled as though it had never happened. I looked at my watch — ten minutes to twelve!

'In ten minutes Robert would enter the room. Thelma would be there also, in answer to my summons, and she would see him murder Paul Conway before her very eyes! Their quarrel downstairs, Robert's assault upon him earlier in the evening — the whole thing fitted in like a jigsaw puzzle. For once fate had been kind to me and presented me with the most perfect design for killing that ever fell to the lot of man!

'Hurriedly putting the body between the bedclothes and switching off the light, I crept out into the corridor. But there another surprise awaited me, for at the head of the stairs I encountered the figure of a man whom I soon found to be no other than my brother Isador! Imploring him to be silent, I led him up to the next floor and into the room formerly occupied by Paul.

'There, having closed the door behind me, I questioned him in whispers about his strange return. His explanation was astonishingly simple: he had come to warn *me*. All night, he said, he'd had a premonition of some imminent danger hanging over me; and when he was seated in his car preparing to drive away, the feeling returned to him more urgently than ever. At last he could endure it no longer, and leaving his car, he walked back towards the house.

'He entered by the west gate and

found, as he'd expected, everything in darkness. He was just about to leave, not wishing to rouse the household, when he noticed that the French windows into the lounge were slightly open. He thereupon made up his mind to enter the house and try, as quietly as possible, to find my bedroom; for the urge to warn me of my danger now seemed absolutely imperative to him.

'So he opened the windows and slipped in. Robert was sitting with his back towards him and didn't take any notice. And thus he proceeded unchallenged until he encountered me at the head of the stairs.

'Having told me this, he asked what I had been doing — for it was obvious by the expression on my face that something out of the ordinary had happened. Indeed, had he but known, it was the sight of him which gave me the greatest shock of the entire evening!

'In short, jerky sentences, I found myself telling him of my crime. And then, after I'd finished, without another word, he left me. He must have slipped down the stairs while you women and Robert were talking outside my room. He went out, I suppose, the same way as he came in — through the lounge.'

'He did,' Tony interrupted. 'It must have been his figure I saw running across the lawn.'

'Then there's no more to be explained. I waited upstairs until you all came and battered on the door. It was then that I was guilty of a gross piece of overacting; for fearful that you might suspect me if I answered at once, I let you knock several times, whereas in reality I'm such a light sleeper that one knock would have been quite sufficient to rouse me. I was surprised when none of you noticed that point.'

'I did,' came from Virginia, 'though I'd forgotten it until now.'

'The rest is simple. I told the inspector a straightforward tale of how Paul had appeared in my room in the middle of the night and asked that we might change over — a statement I knew could be substantiated by the doctor, for it was in front of him that Tony had made the same suggestion in the lounge before dinner.

'So far as Robert was concerned, I jeopardised his position very little, having the uncomfortable feeling that if I was too positive in my evidence against him, I should find myself facing him in court; a situation I was most desirous to avoid, since it would lower my prestige in the esteem of the women for whom I had already gone to such lengths.

'Still, apart from feeling ill and worn out, nothing tangible happened to upset me, until I heard from Thelma that Robert had told her every detail in connection with his visit here in the afternoon. That piece of information put me on my guard. If he'd told Thelma, one might reasonably suppose he'd told the police also; and though the story would sound wild and far-fetched, there was always the possibility, if he were arrested, of their investigating it. And an investigation of these premises would have been the end of me; the contents of that desk alone could have sent me to penal servitude for life.

Therefore, I made up my mind to come

back here tonight, clear up any incriminating evidence there might be lying around, and return home before my absence was discovered. With this idea in view, I managed to get downstairs without being spotted. As I passed the study door, I heard Tony and the inspector talking. There was one tense moment, too, when I saw the sergeant coming up from the servants' quarters; but I contrived to slip out of the front door while he had his back to me.

'I hadn't walked more than ten yards down the drive before I encountered Saunders; I'd brought him down with me that night, knowing that Paul would be staying over the weekend. Saunders always gave me a feeling of security, and I suspected that if Paul at any time became too impossible, Saunders might be easily induced to put him out of the way. For until tonight, I never dreamed that I should be able to adopt that expedient myself, and unaided!

'Saunders had been drawn to the house by the arrival of the police, and was brimming over with curiosity as to what was happening. I told him briefly about Paul being killed — we didn't know by whom — and explained that I was rushing up to town to clear up, in case the police took it into their heads to investigate further afield. Whereupon he immediately suggested he should take my place in bed until my return. I thought the plan an excellent one and gave him my key, having first received his pledge to remain awake and let me in when I returned.

'And so, without more ado, I set off for London. I had not been here long before Virginia arrived. What followed then, you all know.'

With these words, Benjamin concluded his story. The cold light of dawn crept into the room, emphasising their extreme pallor, and they all shivered. Thelma rose to her feet and walked unsteadily over to Robert, who still stood at the same position, with his revolver pointed at Benjamin's heart. Quietly she buried her face against his coat; only by the gentle movements of her shoulders was it possible to discern that she was crying.

Without a word of warning, the silence was rudely shattered. Heavy footsteps sounded from the next room, and through the doorway, accompanied by two constables, together with a man whose face they could not see, came Inspector Coleman. With a grim smile, he crossed to Benjamin. 'Put out your hands,' he snapped.

Looking from the inspector to the two constables, Benjamin realised that to offer any resistance would be useless. Without another word, he held out his hands.

'Thanks for the broadcast,' Coleman rapped out sardonically as he clapped a pair of shining handcuffs on to his wrist. 'That's one of the nicest microphones I've heard for a long while.'

Three pairs of eyes turned towards the microphone as they realised what had happened. But Benjamin's did not; they were fixed upon the man between the two constables who had just raised his head. One word, spoken in a tone of deep regret, rose to his lips: 'Saunders!'

20

On the Roof

'They heard everything, Mr. Fredericks.' Saunders' voice sounded dull and hopeless, as his eyes met Benjamin's.

'And you told them I was here, I suppose?' Benjamin stood swaying slightly backwards and forwards as he spoke, his face quite mask-like in its deathly pallor.

'No, Mr. Fredericks — I didn't tell them anything! It was that doctor — Prescott. He told them.'

'But he didn't know.'

'No, but he told them how he'd seen you out in the garden, and had gone down to follow you. That's what put them on your track. Until then they'd no idea you were missing.'

'That's true enough,' the inspector corroborated. 'You needn't blame your man; he hasn't double-crossed you. Even when we searched the rooms after the others had escaped, he managed to talk in a sleepy kind of voice that sounded like yours.'

'I'm sorry, Saunders.' Benjamin turned to the inspector. 'May I ask what it was that led you here, then? Was it on account of what Robert told you?'

'A good deal of it was. The look of dismay upon this man's face when I said I was coming here was responsible for the rest. When I told him I was bringing him along too, he nearly passed out with fright. Besides all this, your car was traced to the next street where you left it. I heard that by phone, just before we left.'

'I suppose you thought the doctor had taken it?'

'That's right. We got the number from your butler and had you watched by every station all the way down.'

'May I sit down for a moment, Inspector?' Benjamin inquired shakily.

'Certainly.'

He let himself down into the chair, where he sat for several seconds staring before him. 'The doctor! To think that my best friend should be the person to ruin me!'

'He saw you leave and rushed down to stop you. When he found you'd gone, he had the idea that you were off to pay another of your visits to your brother.'

'He warned me not to do that,' muttered Benjamin with the same mirthless smile.

'Knowing how ill you were, he walked over to your brother's to bring you back and also — so he said — to help you get into the house unnoticed.'

'And what did he find at Isador's?'

'He found your brother packing in haste, saying he was leaving the country.'

'He always did hate me,' Benjamin commented.

'And then, as you weren't there, he started to walk back again.'

'And you caught him just as he was about to creep in?'

'Yes.'

'I see. How foolish of me not to have turned off the microphone,' he murmured dreamily.

'Now if you're ready, Mr. Fredericks, we'd better be on the move. I've got a car waiting outside.' The inspector's crisp tones impinged upon his thoughts, making him look up. He looked towards Thelma; but she, unable to bear his gaze, dropped her eyes before him and turned back to Robert.

With a sad smile, Benjamin rose to his feet and took a few steps forward. Slowly, wearily, he tottered across the room until he was standing with his back to the open window. Then with amazing dexterity, he raised his manacled hands and brought them down with all his might upon the inspector's unprotected head. Blinded with pain, Coleman staggered backwards as Benjamin darted onto the fire escape and vanished from sight. Recovering himself almost immediately, the inspector rose to his feet and, shouting to one of the constables to follow him, leapt through the window after him.

Breathless and exhausted, Benjamin struggled up the iron steps. Below him he could hear the inspector's footsteps as he hurled himself forward with his last remaining store of energy. He must reach the top first! He looked over the side and saw his pursuer a couple of landings below. Even in the panic of the moment, he noticed that the inspector's face was covered in blood, as he clung heavily to the railings.

'I must reach the top! I must reach the top!' The words became a frantic hymn as he tottered forward. Now his breath came in short, painful gulps, sticking in his throat. His head was splitting with a rending agony. Still he struggled forward as steps and sky and roofs sought to converge in a shape-less mass before his eyes.

In a haze of exhaustion, he saw the court room, the judge and jury — then the witnesses! Thelma's face, white as death with hollow eyes, appeared before him. No! No, it should never be!

He looked below once more; now only one landing separated them. With a last superhuman effort, he rushed up the few remaining steps and onto the roof. It was now quite light; the clean, cool air, purified by the recent storm, fanned his clammy features as he ran blindly forward. Halfway towards the edge, he heard the inspector as he clattered from the last stair on to the flat roof. This was the crucial moment; whatever happened, he mustn't fail now. Drops of cold sweat appeared upon his brow. Clenching his fists, he threw his whole weight forward. His mouth was wide open; his tortured lungs crying out for air.

With every step, the inspector gained ground, but the race was practically at an end.

At last, with a gasp of relief, Benjamin heaved himself to the edge. For a second he stood poised upon the parapet.

'Stop! Stop!' The cry came from his pursuer, now nearly upon him. But in spite of his nearness, it was too late.

One look from such a dizzy height was all that it required to stop that already overcharged heart; and without using any volition of his own, Benjamin soundlessly crumpled up, and falling off the parapet, hurtled through the air towards the street below!

★　★　★

It was a tired and agitated inspector who, a few minutes later, stumbled back into the room below, prepared to answer the inevitable but unpleasant questions. With a feeling of genuine exhaustion, and from no desire to prevaricate, he asked if he might be permitted a few minutes' grace wherein to seat himself and gather his scattered wits.

The constable who had accompanied him walked with unhurried purposefulness into the black room, whence his footsteps could be heard as he went out into the passage beyond on his way to the front door. The inspector raised his head and looked at the grimly inquisitive faces surrounding him.

'I'm sorry to tell you all that Mr. Fredericks is dead,' he announced.

Silence greeted his statement, which even Thelma, pale but dry-eyed, forbore to break. There are some happenings which are too tragic to call forth a tear, too awe-inspiring to allow any demonstration of grief.

The constable reappeared in the doorway. A look passed between him and the inspector. Then the constable gave a slight nod.

'There's a doctor out there,' he explained in a hushed monotone. 'He says the deceased died instantaneously — several seconds before he reached the ground.'

'Reached the ground?' The query broke from Thelma, in a voice so soft as to be almost inaudible.

'He — threw himself off the roof,' the inspector blurted out in painful embarrassment.

'He did that for us,' she murmured, looking at them all. 'Rather than drag us through the disgrace of a trial, he killed himself. And it was all through me!'

'Thelma, darling!' Leaving Tony, Virginia came to comfort her. But Thelma looked at her with wide expressionless eyes and continued in the same hushed whisper, as though unconscious of any interruption.

'He loved me,' she said in an agonised whisper, 'not as a father loves his daughter — but as he loved my mother. That's why he killed Paul; that's why he wanted to keep me away from Robert.'

'It was wrong, dear, wrong.' Virginia

sought to pacify her, but to no avail; for at that moment no power on earth could have prevented Thelma from voicing the horrible imaginings lurking within her heart.

'That's what you meant, Virginia, when you said you knew why he was playing for time, wasn't it? You thought it was because he couldn't bear to take his eyes off me. That's what you meant, wasn't it?'

Virginia nodded in silence, for she could not deny it.

'Now he's dead; is that my fault too?'

'None of it's your fault, darling. His love for you was wrong; it was wicked. He wasn't normal.'

Thelma looked towards Robert, the tears beginning to gather in her eyes. 'Oh, Robert! I feel so — dreadful.' And with a little sob, she turned her head away.

Robert pacified her as best he could. Now she'd begun to cry, he felt easier in his mind about her and knew the worst was past.

In the meantime, the constable stepped forward. 'Can I do anything about your head, sir?' he inquired of the inspector.

'No — no, I'll get that attended to myself when we reach the station,' Coleman replied impatiently. 'Now you stay here. And you — ' He pointed to the constable who had not left his position beside Saunders. ' — you two come along with me.'

'Are we free to go now?' Tony asked as the inspector rose to his feet.

'Yes. You're free to go, all of you. And next time, young man, take my advice and tell the police the truth. No more stories about cuff links.'

Tony summoned up a ghost of his former grin. 'I hope there won't be any next time, Inspector. But if there is, I promise to take your advice. But how about the inquest? Do you think we shall be needed?'

'That I can't say for the moment,' the inspector answered cautiously. 'But you may be sure that whatever influence I have will be used to keep the whole thing as quiet as possible. And now, if you don't mind, before you leave I should like to know where to find you all, just in case the necessity should arise.'

Robert and Tony thereupon furnished him with their London addresses, which he carefully took down. 'And the ladies?'

Robert tightened his arms around Thelma as he answered softly: 'Won't you leave that to us, Inspector?'

With an understanding look, the inspector shut his notebook and returned it to his pocket. And they all began to walk slowly from the room.

Outside, the sun was shining, while overhead was a clear blue sky without the trace of a cloud anywhere. Early though the hour was, a little crowd had already gathered in the roadway, in the centre of which could be distinguished the white coachwork of an ambulance.

Thelma pressed closer to Robert's side and caught hold of his hand. By this time, the constable had hustled Saunders into the waiting car, while the gallant inspector was not far behind.

Saunders, for his part, remained speechless. When the inspector announced his accomplice's death, he had bowed his head. What his feelings were, none could tell; but as they passed out into the sunshine,

Virginia, being the nearest, stole a glance at his sunken face, and could have sworn that in that brief moment she detected tears in his eyes.

As the inspector gave them a brief nod, the police car started up, passed round the nearest corner, and vanished from their sights.

'I must get to a doctor with this,' said Tony, clutching his shoulder as they walked down to Virginia's car, which stood by the kerb directly in front of them. 'It's getting painful.'

'I'll take you along at once.' Virginia's tone had already assumed that patient maternal note women so often employ when talking to the men of their choice; and she carefully helped him into the car.

Robert and Thelma strolled up the road to where their own car stood, somewhat travel-stained in the keen morning light. The ambulance had slipped away unnoticed, and the crowd also was speedily dispersing. While the car slid gracefully forward, Robert's spirits soared upwards as they had not done for many a day.

'Where do we go to now, Thelma?' he

asked with a joyfulness he was at great pains to disguise.

'Wherever you say, darling,' came her soft reply as she pressed her face gently against his shoulder.

And so with a feeling of happiness and of new responsibility, they drove onward, straight into the heart of the sunrise . . .

Books by Gerald Verner
in the Linford Mystery Library:

THE FACELESS ONES
GRIM DEATH
MURDER IN MANUSCRIPT
THE GLASS ARROW
THE THIRD KEY
THE ROYAL FLUSH MURDERS
THE SQUEALER
MR. WHIPPLE EXPLAINS
THE SEVEN CLUES
THE CHAINED MAN
THE HOUSE OF THE GOAT
THE FOOTBALL POOL MURDERS
THE HAND OF FEAR
SORCERER'S HOUSE
THE HANGMAN
THE CON MAN
MISTER BIG
THE JOCKEY
THE SILVER HORSESHOE
THE TUDOR GARDEN MYSTERY
THE SHOW MUST GO ON
SINISTER HOUSE
THE WITCHES' MOON
ALIAS THE GHOST
THE LADY OF DOOM

THE BLACK HUNCHBACK
PHANTOM HOLLOW
WHITE WIG
THE GHOST SQUAD
THE NEXT TO DIE
THE WHISPERING WOMAN
THE TWELVE APOSTLES
THE GRIM JOKER
THE HUNTSMAN

With Chris Verner:
THE BIG FELLOW
THE SNARK WAS A BOOJUM

We do hope that you have enjoyed reading this large print book.

Did you know that all of our titles are available for purchase?

We publish a wide range of high quality large print books including:

Romances, Mysteries, Classics
General Fiction
Non Fiction and Westerns

Special interest titles available in large print are:

The Little Oxford Dictionary
Music Book, Song Book
Hymn Book, Service Book

Also available from us courtesy of Oxford University Press:

Young Readers' Dictionary
(large print edition)
Young Readers' Thesaurus
(large print edition)

For further information or a free brochure, please contact us at:
Ulverscroft Large Print Books Ltd.,
The Green, Bradgate Road, Anstey,
Leicester, LE7 7FU, England.
Tel: (00 44) 0116 236 4325
Fax: (00 44) 0116 234 0205